NO AWAKENING FI

A blast of cold air hit h
room and into the wall, the torch sweeping
grasp and smashing against the wall.

She tried to get up but the wind was gale force . . . she could not move forward. She could do nothing but stand there, arms and legs spread, starfish-like against the wall, unable to protect herself even as the frost began to form on her clothes, then on her arms and legs, her hands and her face.

She screamed but her voice was a pitiful squeak, lost in the roar of the gale. Then her eyeballs began to ice up. She couldn't close her eyes. She could see the ice forming over the pupils, felt the nip of the frost, saw it happen, watched herself slowly going blind behind a thickening screen of ice, watching herself freeze into oblivion . . .

Also by Gordon McGill:

THE FINAL CONFLICT: OMEN 3
ARMAGEDDON 2000: OMEN 4

Gordon McGill

AMITYVILLE 3-D

Futura
Macdonald & Co
London & Sydney

A Futura Book

First published in Great Britain in 1984
by Futura Publications, a Division of
Macdonald & Co (Publishers) Ltd
London & Sydney

ISBN 0 7088 2471 4

Typeset, printed and bound in Great Britain by
Hazell Watson & Viney Limited,
Member of the BPCC Group,
Aylesbury, Bucks

Futura Publications
A Division of
Macdonald & Co (Publishers) Ltd
Maxwell House
74 Worship Street
London EC2A 2EN
A BPCC plc Company

Dino de Laurentiis presents
a Richard Fleischer Film

AMITYVILLE 3-D

Starring Tony Roberts, Tess Harper, Robert Joy and Candy Clark as Melanie
With John Beal, Leora Dana, John Harkins, Lori Loughlin, Meg Ryan, Neill Barry and Pete Kowanko
Music by Howard Blake
Film Editor Frank J. Urioste A.C.E.
Director of Photography Fred Schuler
Written by William Wales
Produced by Stephen F. Kesten
Directed by Richard Fleischer

ONE

It was a perfect night, thought Caswell, for calling up the dead. The sky was black and heavy with thunder clouds. Ragged oak trees creaked in the wind and, above the door, a peeling FOR SALE sign squeaked in its bracket. Caswell glanced at it. The man who put it up was a supreme optimist. No one had lived in the house for years or even within half a mile of it, nor was anyone likely to . . . you'd have to be crazy to live in 112 Ocean Avenue, Amityville.

Slowly, with the gait of a cripple, he shuffled down the three steps from the doorway to the drive and looked up at the place. It was a large, rambling house, three storeys of clapboard. From the outside it was a typical Long Island family home. He turned and stared down the garden towards the river. It was high summer but there was not a single leaf on the trees. Once, someone had planted tulips at the feet of plaster statues of the saints. The flowers had died, black rashers for leaves, crushed, rotting bulbs.

A perfect night and a perfect location.

He checked his watch and looked up at the attic windows, two of them, half-moon shapes. The attic light was on and the windows reminded him of eyes. No matter where you went in sight of the house, the eyes seemed to be watching you, like medieval portraits, following you wherever you went.

They should be here by now. He tried to remember

the man's name but couldn't. It had been a typical phone call. The man had tried to sound flippant, had attempted to keep the anxiety from his voice, but he had failed. The men never wanted to admit that they needed his kind of help. It was somehow considered unmasculine to ask for the assistance of a medium. It was always the last resort, when all else had failed. He had come up with the usual excuse. It was for the sake of his wife. How many times had he heard that line, but it gave the poor souls a measure of self-respect.

Now he could hear the car, saw the beam of light coming out of Coles Avenue. He hobbled up the steps and waited. The car swung into the drive and he shielded his eyes from the headlights. It came to a halt a few yards from the main door and the engine was killed, the lights turned off. Now the only sound was the wind. For a full minute the occupants sat where they were. Caswell could see them talking. One of them, he reckoned, was scared to come out. He or she was having last minute doubts.

The driver's door opened and the man got out. Medium height, curly haired, stocky; about forty, Caswell thought. Then the woman. Caswell nodded in appreciation. She looked around twenty-five, dark, slim, big brown eyes and, for the thousandth time in his life, Caswell cursed his ugliness. He was well aware that he repelled people. He had a face like a prune, a body that looked as though it had been assembled by a drunk.

He saw the woman pull her coat tightly round her body and touch her bag, a large traveller's bag. Briefly Caswell wondered why she had brought such a hefty piece of luggage, then he stepped back as the man came towards him, unsmiling. The woman followed, glanced at the attic and made an instinctive sign of the Cross. The two men shook hands and Caswell stood back to let them enter, heaved the heavy door shut, pushing hard against the force of the wind, then smiled at them, trying to appear reassuring.

The man introduced his wife. Melanie. Caswell shook hands, noted the brief expression of distaste, quickly smothered. They gazed around the empty house and he felt their confusion. It was bare of furnishing, bare floorboards, the staircase rough and peeling. Faded rectangles chased one another up the stairs, reminders of past owners and their prints and paintings.

'We only use the house for our sittings,' he said by way of explanation. 'We have a cottage nearby.'

Melanie was not interested. She gazed at him imploringly, the strong face creased with tension.

'Mr Caswell, can you really help us?' It was a plea for reassurance.

'I believe we can,' he said, making no move to show them further into the house. He was waiting for something. Suddenly the man nodded, reached into his pocket, drew out an envelope and handed it over. Caswell pocketed it without a word, then led them to a door on the left of the hall. The boards creaked as the others followed, Melanie glancing up the stairs, at light bulbs with empty sockets, windows without curtains, It was impersonal, about as welcoming as Alcatraz.

Caswell ushered them into the living room and stood back to let them take a good look. It was a big room, the width of the house, over thirty feet and looked bigger, being so sparsely furnished. There was only one round table with four chairs. The floorboards were bare, the fireplace blocked up. Two spindly lamps stood in opposite corners, each giving out faint haloes of yellow light. There was a door in the far wall leading to the porch. Opposite, in the right hand corner, another door, half open, showing a staircase leading to the cellar. The windows were covered by thick grey curtains which reached the floor.

Like the rest of the house, the room was cold and depressing.

'Please,' said Caswell, to Melanie, indicating one of the chairs. She moved towards it then stopped, startled by a deep voice bidding good evening. Framed in the porch door was a small woman holding a black candle.

'My wife Emma,' said Caswell. 'Mr and Mrs Baxter.'

She looked ill; pale and thin, the face of a bird, white hair scraped back into a bun, her eyes rheumy, the skin stretched across the cheekbones, laced with tiny veins. Baxter nodded to her, thinking she could do with a blood transfusion, but when she smiled, her expression changed, a gentle smile of reassurance. She took Melanie's hand and led her to the table, sat next to her. Baxter followed them and took his seat, still anxious, the tension surrounding him like static electricity.

'You're sure there's no danger,' he said to Caswell. 'I mean, after all that's happened in this house. People driven out. That family murdered . . .'

Caswell shook his head, smiled as though talking to a child. 'The house itself is not an evil place. But there is some power here, centred on the earth . . .'

'Evil or good,' said his wife, interrupting him, 'lie in our response.'

Baxter shrugged. There was no answer to that, nothing more to say. It was time to get on with it, for better or worse. He sat next to Melanie, squeezed her shoulder. She looked up at him, puppy-like, a nervous smile fluttering, her eyes bright.

'Shall we begin?' Emma had taken charge of the proceedings. Caswell snapped out the lights, came back to the table and lit the candle. The flame rose two inches, a perfect tulip shape, untouched by draught. The wind battered at the windows but found no entry. The only sound was a shutter somewhere, banging against a wall.

'Please place your hands on the table,' Caswell whispered.

They did as they were asked.

'We must establish a chain.'

Baxter felt Melanie's fingers on his. His left hand was grasped by Caswell, the fingers damp. Baxter had once picked up a grass snake. The feeling was similar. He shivered involuntarily and looked across the table. Emma had closed her eyes.

'Concentrate on your child,' she muttered, the sound hoarse and guttural. Her voice had changed. Baxter felt a tremor run up his back. Melanie's fingers tightened. The others had closed their eyes now but Baxter continued to stare round the room, searching for something. Caswell nudged him and he bowed his head, eyelids fluttering, the table a blur, white fingers interlacing across the pine.

'Call to him, Mrs Baxter,' said Emma. 'Call to your child. Let him know you're here.'

Baxter felt Melanie's fingers flutter. There was no sound. He turned and snatched a glance at her. She was gasping, trying to say something. Her lips trembled but she could make no sound.

Another exhortation from Emma. Melanie opened

her eyes. He smiled at her in encouragement. She swallowed, tried again.

'Ricky, it's Mommy.' A squeak of a voice. 'Ricky, can you hear me?'

Silence like a fog. No answer. No response of any kind. Caswell's hand tightened on Baxter's. Melanie grabbed his wrist. He felt their sweat mingle. He began to shiver and realized it was more than the tension. He was cold. He glanced at the candle, saw the flame flicker and almost die. Their shadows danced. The wind was with them in the room now, whining at them.

There was a new sound, a grunt like a wounded bull. Baxter turned and gazed in horrified fascination at Emma. Her head had fallen back. Her throat pulsed, a scrawny turkey-neck, Adam's apple trembling. She moaned, low as if in terrible pain, the sound rising to a wail. Baxter stared at her. She did not stop for breath. A full minute, then two, wailing, a high pitched howl of a banshee. Then she was answered by a small voice, that of a child, a sad child, sobbing quietly.

Emma's eyes opened, bulging, staring sightlessly at the ceiling. Then, without warning, she screamed. Baxter felt Melanie trying to rise but Emma held her tightly, forcing her to remain seated. He looked round the room but could see nothing, only their shadows.

He strained to listen. The wind had risen. Emma's breathing was a heavy death rattle. He felt himself breathing in rhythm, along with Caswell and Melanie, all of them gasping for breath, lungs pumping in harmony. The room was alive with the sound, a throbbing, pulsing rhythm. It was as if something were struggling to be born . . .

Melanie was staring around the room, neck muscles

taut, the tendons like barbed wire. Baxter felt that if her hands were not held, she would spin off into the air like an escaping balloon. Suddenly the panting eased, to become an indistinct whisper, one voice breathing lightly, gradually becoming distinct. A question. 'Where?' it asked. A single syllable, a repetitive exhalation of breath, surrounding them, coming at them from the four corners of the room.

Emma's lips moved but there was no sound. The voice did not belong to her.

'We're here,' murmured Caswell, repeating the phrase in a dull monotone. 'Come through,' he coaxed. 'We're waiting . . . come through . . .'

Emma's head rolled as if her neck had been snapped. Her face was a horror mask of fear. Her eyes were open but saw nothing, unfocused, staring blindly, the pupils moving at random as if her brain had lost the ability to control them.

'Can't breathe,' she said, a rasping sound, a grunt. 'No air. I need help. Help me. Smoke. Fire . . .'

Her eyes glazed over and her lips spread in a rictus grin, the teeth clamped together. Her back arched and she seemed to snarl. It was the face of an animal, snarling and spitting, gasping for breath. Baxter lost track of time, staring at her as she writhed in her chair, then he sat back startled as she slumped forward, her head cracking against the table. The pulsing died, leaving silence. The candle burned brightly again and true, without interference.

'The child has passed over,' said Emma, sitting upright, eyes closed. 'The child has passed over in fire. Now he is at peace.'

Silence. Baxter glanced at Melanie, heard the hiss of

a sob, saw her shoulders heave, then the candle went out and they were in total darkness.

Baxter had had enough but he stayed where he was. It wasn't time. For a full minute they sat in silence, no one moving. The noise when it came was unexpected and he twitched, heard Melanie gasp in fear. A crash beneath them, wood on wood. Twice. The table trembled and began to move, rising an inch, then further until it swayed a foot from the ground. He rose with it, in a crouch, then forced himself back into his chair as Caswell yelled at him not to move, whatever you do, don't move.

He looked around but his eyes had still not adjusted to the dark. He could see nothing. The only sound was a deep voice, indistinct, an angry voice muttering, the sound wafting around them. Emma began to writhe as if something were pulling her.

'Go,' yelled Caswell into the darkness. 'Go. Leave us . . .' A wild exhortation. He grabbed Baxter's hand, the grip stronger than the puny frame seemed to allow. Again he roared at the voice, striving for authority.

Silence once more. Emma shuddered, released from the grip. Darkness and silence, then punctuated by the crying of a child.

'Ricky,' Melanie moaned, tried to stand but Emma held her down.

'Stay where you are,' said Caswell sharply. Baxter leant towards her, whispered her name. She shook her head, murmuring the name, again and again.

'Mommy, I'm here . . .'

Each head turned towards the sound. In one corner of the ceiling above the porch door, a small patch of light had appeared. The voice came at them from the centre, faint, a stuttering plea. 'I'm here, Mommy . . . here.'

The light moved towards them, flickered, almost down towards the table until it was only two feet from Melanie's face. She stared at it, tried to reach out for it, but her hands were held against the table. She moaned deep in her throat as it moved away towards the hall door, fading as it went.

'Stay, please,' she whispered.

Caswell shook his head. 'It's only beginning,' he said softly.

Now they could hear footsteps, a soft tip-tap in the hall, short steps, the sound of a child running. Melanie blinked as the light reappeared over the table then drifted again towards the hall. They gazed at it, Baxter and Melanie unable to grasp what they were seeing, unable to comprehend the fact that the light was slowly but gradually taking on a shape, forming into thc shimmering outline of a child, a boy of about five, smiling at them.

Baxter grunted an obscenity and turned abruptly as Melanie kicked back her chair and reached for her bag.

'No,' Caswell yelled, his voice almost drowning the screech of terror from Emma.

'You'll kill the medium.' He lunged for Melanie but Baxter pushed him away, jumping to his feet as the room exploded in a starburst of white light. Everyone except Melanie blinked involuntarily, temporarily blinded. A half-second of blackness, then a second flash, followed by a third. Caswell stood up, open mouthed, at Melanie who was crouched low, the camera at her face, the strobe unit setting off a series of flashes, exposing a youth by the door. He was dressed in a hooded black leotard, his face, darkened by charcoal. He held a luminous piece of cardboard in the shape of a child. He was motionless, open-mouthed like Caswell.

Baxter hit the light switch and grinned at Caswell. Emma was screaming; a thin sound, ignoring her husband's demands to shut her goddamned mouth. The little man turned and glared at Baxter, fists clenched, his face a comic mask of indignation.

'You have no right!' He spluttered over the phrase as if there was a blockage in his throat.

The youth was the first to react, dropping the cardboard cut-out and rushing at Melanie, bunching his fist for a punch but he was clumsy; an amateur. Baxter did not even have to take a step forward. He simply drove an elbow into the skinny abdomen as the youth rushed past him, watching him go down, retching into the floorboards.

As he leant over him, the basement door was pushed wide open and a girl in jeans and T-shirt rushed through the room towards the hall, grimly determined to get out of the house. Baxter stepped back to allow Melanie a clear view. The motordrive whirred and she got her pictures, each one of the charlatans exposed in Nikon.

It was almost over; a few more snaps of Caswell snarling defiance, of Emma in hysterics, and all that remained was to listen to the protests.

'Who are you?' squealed Caswell. 'What do you want?' The questions were feeble protests from a defeated man.

Baxter reached into his pocket and pulled out a business card, held it in front of Caswell's face.

'*Witness Magazine*,' he said. 'Congratulations. You've just made our next cover.'

Caswell shook his head as if he had taken a heavy punch. His mouth opened and shut and Baxter was reminded of a fish flapping on a slab.

'You've no right. You can't . . .' It was the same squeak he had conjured up for the seance but now it was legitimate.

'No right?' said Baxter. 'No right? We've got pictures,' he nodded towards Melanie.

'Plus. We've got sound.' He opened his jacket to reveal a tape recorder. 'And,' he winked, 'we've got you. All of you.'

Caswell blinked. 'Get out,' he said weakly, trying to think of something that might salvage a piece of the evening. 'You're trespassing.' It was all he could think of.

'Actually,' said Melanie. 'We've taken care of that.' She looked beyond him, out of the door towards the hall where Baxter was headed. 'Wait for it,' she said.

Baxter opened the front door and stood back to let two men come in. The first was in his thirties, small boned and delicate, the other a man in his fifties, tall, white haired, both wearing expensive suits, both the essence of respectability. Caswell could think of nothing except to attack.

'Who's this? More trash from your goddam scandal sheet?'

Baxter indicated the younger man. 'Mr Caswell, let me introduce Dr Elliot West of the Institute of Psychic Research, State University, Long Island.'

Caswell was unimpressed. 'I don't give a damn where he's from,' he sneered. 'I'm gonna sue the ass offa you and every sonofabitch connected with you.'

Baxter ignored him. 'And this,' he said, bringing the

second newcomer into the room, 'is Mr Carl Wunch of the District Attorney's office . . .'

Caswell swore beneath his breath.

'We took the liberty of informing him of our plans and he's been good enough to come along tonight.'

Wunch stared hard at Caswell as Baxter continued. 'If you have any questions regarding the law . . . ?'

He reached out towards Caswell, lifted the envelope from his back pocket, the one he had given him half an hour earlier. Caswell made a grab for it, but he was too late.

'Like I say,' continued Baxter, 'any questions, I suggest you talk to him.'

He handed the envelope to Wunch who opened it, counted ten 50-dollar bills, then slipped the envelope into his pocket.

Caswell hopped from foot to foot. 'Conducting a seance isn't a crime,' he said.

Wunch sniffed. 'We call it fraud,' he said.

Caswell puffed his cheeks, glanced over Wunch's shoulder at the youth who had dragged himself to the door and was propped against the wall, clutching the piece of cardboard.

Caswell was beaten and he knew it. He turned and yelled at his wife, then pushed past Baxter towards the door. Emma followed him, her face white with shock; real shock, no longer simulated. The youth dragged himself to his feet and staggered into the hallway, each step of his retreat being photographed by Melanie. As the woman passed in front of the viewfinder, Melanie caught the look of hatred. She lowered the camera. Emma hawked up phlegm and spat in her face. Melanie shuddered and stepped back, bumping into the table, wiped her face with her sleeve as the woman stalked after her husband. It was the final obscenity.

Baxter put his arm round her and asked her if she was okay. She nodded and began packing her camera away, unscrewing the lens. She'd had enough for the night. He kissed her lightly on the top of the head then turned and followed Caswell out of the house, standing in the drive watching the four of them trudging down the path, the cardboard child being dragged upside down, glowing in the night air. As they vanished down Ocean Avenue, the child was the only reminder of the seance, a cardboard ghost, walking on its head, smiling farewell at him.

Back in the house, West was reluctant to leave. He wanted to take a look around.

'Sure,' said Baxter. 'We've got to get some shots of their equipment. Haven't we, Melanie?'

She shrugged at him and began unpacking her camera again. She wasn't thrilled at the idea of hanging around. She'd rather have come back in the morning and done the job in daylight. But if Baxter wanted it done, then okay. He was the boss. West was happily surveying the place, looking in corners. He turned and called out to Baxter that the master control would probably be in the basement.

They moved in single file to the basement door, Baxter in the lead. Without warning the lights went out. Baxter banged into something and swore. He could hear Melanie gasp, catch her breath, felt her hand on his arm, then a light flickered on. It was West, holding up his lighter, his face suddenly anxious. Baxter rubbed his head and looked at his fingers, smeared in blood.

'Fusebox?' asked West.

'Must have been,' said Baxter, feeling the wall.

'Or worse,' said Melanie, her voice a nervous squeak.

West held the lighter out. Lit from below, Melanie looked haggard and Baxter was reminded of the old Hallowe'en trick of holding a candle under your chin and seeing your reflection in the mirror, frightening yourself with a vision of the future, seeing yourself as an old man . . .

'The way the storm's been blowing,' Melanie said, 'there could be lines down.'

West nodded. 'Maybe we should . . .'

'Leave?' Melanie finished the sentence. It was more than a suggestion. She was pleading.

They climbed into their cars in a hubbub of goodbyes, thank yous and vows to meet soon. Melanie glanced up at the house and thought she saw movement. It was a fly, settling on the windowsill of the bedroom on the second floor. It gazed down at them, unmoving, a fat housefly, staring at them as they left, tyres screeching on gravel, tail lights fading into the distance, and still it remained unmoving even as the window began slowly to frost over, ferns of ice, interlocking, obscuring the view, a jungle of frost, and the fly still watched, as if on guard, fat and succulent on the frosted window pane.

The drive back to Manhattan took an hour but to Baxter it seemed longer. He'd wanted to listen to a baseball game on the radio but there was too much static. It was everywhere. He couldn't get one station; and Melanie didn't help. She hardly uttered a word until they went through the Holland Tunnel. It was unlike her. Normally she was a talker, perhaps too much, always chattering about anything. You couldn't get a word in edgeways. But that night she was silent. It wasn't until he dropped her off at her apartment in the Village that she smiled and said goodnight.

'I thought you were great tonight,' he said.

'Thanks.'

'I liked the sobbing. You coulda got an Oscar for the sobbing.'

She smiled at him and waved as he drove uptown. She couldn't tell him that the sobbing had been for real. She couldn't tell a professional sceptic like John Baxter that she had experienced something horrible, that, before the farce of the cardboard child, she had turned ice cold and become aware of . . . what was the word the mediums used . . . ? A presence, that was it. If she had been asked to describe it, she would have been in trouble. There was no shape, nothing physical to describe, just a feeling of something ultimately evil, and angry, something that wanted to hurt her.

TWO

Trevor Sanders was sweating as he drove into Amityville. He always seemed to be sweating these days. Every pore seeped. His palms slipped on the steering wheel. It was worry; that and his obesity, a lousy combination. He could feel his heart batter against his rib cage and he thought back a couple of days to his doctor's warning.

'Screw him,' he said aloud. 'It's my body. It's my lousy pump. If it's gonna go, it's gonna go. Screw it.'

He glanced at his watch as he turned the station wagon into Ocean Avenue. Just time to check out number 112 before lunch. He promised himself a big lunch and a coupla beers. Screw the doctor, he said again.

There was a red Ford in the driveway, with an Avis sticker on the windscreen. Sanders glanced at it, heaved himself out of the driving seat and ambled to the door, fumbling for the right key. The FOR SALE sign creaked above him and he cursed it.

He hated this house, hated himself for his stupidity in buying it. It was a burden, three storeys of white elephant. If only someone would come along who didn't know its history, but that was too much to ask. Everyone knew about the Amityville horror house. You'd have had to be from Mars not to know about it, he grumbled. Talking to himself again. He was going nuts. What he needed was to find someone who didn't give a damn about things that went bump in the night, someone without a trace of superstition. That's who he needed.

He stood in the hall and looked around.

'Anyone here?' his voice echoed around the bare rooms. No answer. They were probably out by the river, he thought. He looked into the living room, trying to think what it would look like with a bit of paint, the boards sanded and varnished. It would be a nice place to live, well worth the price he was asking . . .

His thoughts were interrupted by the sound of a man in pain. Sanders shuddered, and held on to the door for support. He gazed round the room. It was empty.

'Oh Jesus,' he muttered, clutching at his chest, feeling his heart thump. He wanted to turn and run but his legs would not obey the signals from his brain. He was staring at the far corner of the room when a movement distracted him. He blinked. The table was moving. It rose a few inches then crashed back on to the boards, raising dust.

'Oh Christ.' He thought he was going to faint, felt his knees buckle. He blinked again. A broom handle had appeared through a gap in the floorboards. He bent low and stared at it, bewildered but no longer terrified. Someone was in the basement playing games.

'Help me.' A voice echoed through the room. Sanders spun on one heel. He was alone, with a disembodied voice. 'Help me. I'm being held prisoner.'

He whimpered like a puppy, the fear rising in him once more like bile.

'Who would want you?' This time the voice was female, a Brooklyn accent.

The he saw a Bakelite speaker, half concealed behind a curtain, a wire trailing along the skirting boards, and the fear subsided again.

'Hey,' the woman again. 'Get your hand offa my ass.'

'That's not my hand,' said the male.

Sanders blew bad air, puffing like a whale, then grinned to himself and wiped the sweat from his brow as the speaker erupted into shrieks and giggles.

He moved to the basement door and slowly made his way down the stairs, stopped half-way and peered into the gloom. It was a big room and Sanders knew the measurements off by heart. Forty-three feet by twenty-eight with a smaller playroom to his left, wood panelled with a dropped ceiling. Shafts of sunlight sliced down from the barred windows at ground level, painting a zebra pattern on Melanie.

Sanders leered at her. She was his kind of woman. A looker. It was a pity that she wasn't alone. For a moment he watched her taking pictures of the man who was jiggling the broom handle through a gap in the ceiling. Behind him a sound system had been set up, a microphone and amplifiers, wires trailing up to the ceiling.

Sanders lumbered down the remaining steps, offering a cheery hallo.

They turned and looked at him, unsmiling.

'Mr Sanders?' said Baxter.

'That's me. Trevor George Sanders.' He spread his hands wide. 'Proud owner of this palace.'

He gazed at the equipment and shook his head. 'I'll tell you this. When I rented the house to those people I sure had no idea they were up to anything like this. When you phoned, it was quite a shock.'

Baxter nodded. The man was lying. He was already offering a defence when no attack had been made.

'Thanks for letting us come over,' he said.

'No problem.' Sanders shook hands, winked at Melanie. She winked back. He picked up the broom handle and began poking it at the ceiling.

'Some box of tricks, huh?'

No reply. They weren't being friendly. He began to sweat again. What he didn't need was to get involved with nosy reporters with no sense of humour.

He stepped back and at first he thought they were pulling some stunt on him as a floorboard snapped with a crack like a pistol shot. His left foot slipped through the gap and he toppled sideways, flailing at air, trying to grab something, his shin scraping against the jagged wood, his knee lodging beween two boards. He swore, felt foolish, tried to get up, then squealed as a second board snapped under his weight and he began slithering into a void, his hands scrabbling for a grip, a scream building in his throat as a third board snapped. The room spun and he thought he could see a fly on the banister, a fat housefly, its wings sparkling as if sprinkled with icing, then his arm was grabbed and Baxter was shouting at him to hold on.

For a moment he thought he was a dead man. He could feel himself slithering into oblivion, then Melanie grabbed his other arm and he was pulled up and heaved on to the floor, where he lay panting like a beached whale.

Four boards had snapped. Slowly he dragged himself upright, aware that he had been muttering obscenities. He apologized to Melanie who simply shrugged at him as if to say, so what? She'd heard a lot worse.

Baxter was on his knees, pulling the boards up and gazing into a hole, four feet in diameter.

'I guess this is what's supposed to be the gateway to hell,' he said.

'Looks pretty convincing,' said Melanie.

Sanders shook his head. 'Just an old dry well,' he said, peering down cautiously over Baxter's shoulder. The sides were bricked up and damp. Weeds sprouted through crumbling mortar. He couldn't see the bottom.

'Ain't in the plans,' he said, but he was talking to himself. Baxter had got up and gone to the stairs, and when Sanders turned to follow him, he found himself staring into the lens of Melanie's Nikon. He raised his arms to cover his face, like an Arab whose soul was in danger.

'Don't do that,' he yelled. 'That's not for your magazine, is it?'

'Do you have any objections?' asked Baxter.

'Damn right. If it makes me look like I was part of this charade . . .'

'According to Caswell, you were.' Baxter delivered the accusation like a prosecuting attorney and Sanders stepped back, almost stumbled a second time into the well, protesting his innocence, saying that Caswell was a goddamned lying bastard.

Melanie caught him again with the Nikon, and again as he moved towards Baxter.

'You don't believe that runt, do you?'

Baxter said nothing. There was a moment of silence, a stand-off as the two men stared at one another, then Sanders nodded towards the door.

'Let's go out,' he said. 'I need some air.' He had started to sweat again.

Melanie watched them through the viewfinder,

tracked them as they went upstairs, Baxter in the lead, the fat behind of Sanders wobbling after him. She snapped a couple more shots, grinned and lowered the camera, then grimaced. The air in the room was bad. She wasn't sure if it was the well or Sanders; either way she agreed with the fat man. She wanted out.

For ten minutes she wandered round the house, seeing it through the viewfinder, discovering the place, square by square. She didn't like it. She was still uneasy. Maybe it was the memory of the previous night. Maybe it was the knowledge of the house's history. She wasn't sure. All she knew was that she was uncomfortable, and cold in the height of summer. The place gave her the shivers. Literally.

She moved up the stairs to the first floor, running her hand along the banister and flinching as she touched something. She shuddered in disgust. She hated flies, always had. She lowered the camera and watched it zip in circles in front of her, going upstairs with her, almost as if it were leading her somewhere. She shook her head, cursed her stupid imagination. The boards on the staircase creaked. Some of them needed replacing. Anyone moving around would make a hell of a din in the middle of the night, and she remembered the story all those years ago of the young man who had murdered his family with a rifle, and she wondered how he could have done it. The mother and father, two sisters, two brothers, all shot through the head, all lying face down. How could he have done it? Surely after the first shot, the others would have wakened?

He'd been possessed. That was one theory. She shuddered. It didn't bear thinking about.

She stopped at the first floor landing and opened the door on her right. It squeaked as it swung open, showing a bare room. It was dark, the shutters closed. She screwed on her flash and hit the shutter button. Briefly the room was lit up, a blank featureless place. She was aware of something in the frame and looked up. The fly buzzed in front of her. She flapped a hand at it and moved to the window, opened the shutters. A gauze curtain fluttered as the summer sun flooded in. Something tickled her hair and again she flapped at the fly, cursing it, telling it to get the hell away from her, then placed her elbows on the sill and leaned out.

The garden ran a hundred feet to a boathouse and a small jetty that jutted into the Amityville River. It should have been an idyllic spot. All it needed was the laughter of children, the smell of a barbecue maybe. But there was nothing. It was a dead place. All the houses nearby were shuttered and closed, a cemetery of real estate. What was it Baxter had said yesterday? No one would live within sight of the house, an acre of desolation in what should have been high-rent accommodation.

She spotted movement by the boathouse, picked up the camera, fitted a powerful lens and focused on the two figures that came into view. Baxter's expression was aloof, giving nothing away. Sanders was anxious, gesticulating, perspiring. If the fat man were in on the action, she thought, then Baxter would get him and draw him into the web. If there was one species of humanity that John Baxter despised it was the exploiter of grief. She focused on Sanders's lips and wondered what he was saying . . .

He was still protesting his innocence.

'Where does that penny ante con man get off accusing me?' he asked between swipes at the sweat on his brow.

'Don't know about penny ante,' said Baxter. 'They must have pulled in quite a haul over the last six months.'

'Well, it's nothing to do with me. You can't possibly connect me. There's not a shred of proof.'

Baxter grunted. Proof, indeed. As soon as someone mentioned proof, he or she was usually involved. Innocent people don't mention proof.

Sanders was staring at him, waiting for a response, but he got none. Baxter just kept walking. For a moment, Sanders stopped, stared at the other man's back, then mopped his brow and trotted after him like a pregnant sow; a man bathed in anxiety.

'Look, Mr Baxter,' he said catching up, puffing halitosis at him. 'You know my profession. I'm in real estate. Just take a glance at this.' He fished in his jacket pocket and pulled out a cyclostyled leaflet, a smudgy picture of the house, taken from the river bank.

'Okay, what we have here is a six bedroom house built in 1928. Dutch Colonial style. Six bedrooms, living room, dining room, three bathrooms, large garage with space for two cars, swimming pool and boathouse.'

Baxter squinted at him, wondering why he was getting the sales pitch. Sanders held up a hand to silence any objections and continued reading.

'You got a piece of land, fifty feet by two-forty, your own jetty into the Amityville River. The ocean's only a few minutes away. It's a prime site. Okay?'

Baxter nodded.

'Listen. You know about the real estate business. I do a lot of work in this area. I've a reputation to protect.

If I get somehow tied up with this Caswell business nonsense, I could be finished.'

Nothing from Baxter. He remained expressionless, waiting for Sanders to continue.

'I bought the house cheap because I figured it would be a good investment once all the panic was forgotten. Trouble is, it's never been forgotten. I can't even unload the houses around it.'

He flapped a podgy hand south towards Coles Avenue. Baxter followed his gaze. There were empty houses all around, some with boarded up windows. It was a silent area. No sign of life. No birds, no hum of insects. Nothing. He turned and looked at the river. Probably no fish either. It was as if it had been visited by plague.

Sanders continued talking, fast, as if to stop too long would let Baxter in with some accusation or other.

'It's an ordinary, normal house, nice looking, relatively good condition, built the way they used to build them. It's a steal. And nobody wants it.'

Baxter glanced back at it. A cloud broke up and the place was suddenly awash in sunlight, picking out the dark blue shingles and the white edging.

'And to think,' said Sanders. 'It was once called High Hopes. The sign's still there in the driveway. Christ. High fuckin' Hopes, indeed.'

Baxter turned, startled by the unexpected obscenity. 'What are you asking for it?'

Sanders smiled, a face filled with relief. 'Well, let's just say it will be affordable. Very affordable.'

He moved closer, whispered at Baxter. 'Leave me out of your story and I'll give you almost any terms you want.'

A movement in the house caught his eye. Melanie

was standing at a second storey window, her camera at her face. That would be the sewing room, he thought, the bedroom of the young man who went crazy and murdered his family. He waved. Melanie waved back. He could hear Sanders panting at his shoulder and he moved away from him. Normally the plea to be kept out of a story landed the person deeper into it, but he had decided yesterday that Sanders could not be mentioned. There was no proof. The only link was Caswell and he was the villain of the piece. His word was worthless. Were Sanders to appear in *Witness*, he would be able to sue the magazine into backruptcy. But the fat man didn't know that, and besides, there was an additional factor to be taken into account. He had fallen in love with 112 Ocean Avenue.

He turned and said something that would make Trevor Sanders the happiest real estate man in Long Island.

'How much is affordable?'

Melanie had run out of film. She turned away from the window, packing her camera into its case. Again she was aware of the fly, gently doing laps of the room before coming to a stop on a patch of sunlight on the wall. She turned back to check that Baxter was coming back and blinked, puzzled. The window was closed, but she couldn't remember closing it. It had been open a moment ago, the curtain flapping in the breeze. She shrugged. She was getting absent-minded. Only the other day she had gone to the bedroom for something, forgotten what it was, then did the old trick of retracing her steps to the point where she had gone up to the kitchen and couldn't remember what she was doing there . . . Old age. At twenty-five. Premature senility.

As she turned away from the window, the fly zipped into her face. She ducked and swiped at it. Briefly it hovered like a hornet, a few inches from her eyes, close enough so that she could see the little fluted proboscis. She stared at the eyes and remembered an old horror film she had seen, about a scientist who had broken himself down into atoms and transported himself across his laboratory; the only problem was that a fly had got into the machine and when the atoms reassembled, the scientist had the head and the arm of the fly, and his head was buzzing around somewhere with the fly's body.

She remembered the scene from the fly's point of view, hundreds of images. She swiped at it again and it flew to the ceiling. Again she glanced at the window. Sure as hell couldn't remember closing it. She was cold again. Freezing. As she went downstairs she rubbed at the gooseflesh on her arms.

Baxter and Sanders were talking in the driveway. She went straight to the car and waited for them, glad to be out of the house. She saw Sanders wave and heave himself into the station wagon. Baxter grinned at her, gave her a conspiratorial wave, then did a strange thing. He locked the front door of the house and patted the lintel, ran his fingers over the small banister that ran up the three steps.

Why on earth would he pat a house? Melanie shook her head. The job was getting to be too much for him.

THREE

The story had taken an hour to write. It was simplicity itself, the best sort of story, exposing charlatans. He pecked out a line on his typewriter, the sort of line he had written before with much pleasure: '*Witness Magazine* yesterday handed over the file on the Caswells to the local district attorney's office.' Now it was up to Wunch to decide whether or not there would be a prosecution.

West had been commissioned to write an accompanying piece on the house. It was always a good move to get the experts in on the act; it added to the credibility of the story. Carefully he checked his copy. He had written a few lines on the history of the house, how on the night of November 13th, 1974 a certain Ronald DeFeo had taken a .35 calibre Marlin rifle and murdered his family. Ronald Snr, his wife Louise, Dawn and Allison, Mark and John, each shot in the head while they slept on their stomachs.

DeFeo had confessed forty hours later and was eventually sentenced to 150 years, six consecutive terms of 25 years. Baxter had added that later there was some controversy over the case, that it had been suggested that he was under some sort of spiritual possession when he committed the killings; and the fact that no one had heard the shots had never been satisfactorily explained.

He had then added a few lines about the family who

had moved into the house over a year later. They had lasted only twenty-eight days then ran, leaving everything behind, claiming it was an evil place where dreadful inexplicable things had happened. Baxter had been tempted at first to add some of the stories: how the woman found her lavatory bowls blackened, that objects had moved mysteriously, doors had been wrenched from their frames, a crucifix had been turned upside down, that a priest who had tried to help had become violently ill and stigmata had appeared on his hands, that the owners had suffered obscene hallucinations . . .

It was a long list and Baxter had ignored it. The stories would detract from the main point which was the exposé of the Caswells. It was old hat now anyway, and frankly, Baxter did not believe a word of it. He had seen too many charlatans and too many hoaxes; and he was a born sceptic. Even as a child he had questioned everything, demanded rational explanations. His mother often told her friends of a thunderstorm when he was three, how she had tried to calm his fears with the old tale of God moving the furniture around and how he had looked at her as if she were quite mad.

As a young reporter he had been involved in a particularly nasty hoax. He had believed it was real, he'd been taken in by the perpetrators, so that, when it was proved to be a con, his scepticism was reinforced, like a bone which, having been fractured, resets stronger than before.

Now no one would pull the wool over his eyes. To John Baxter, there was a rational explanation for everything. Anyone who thought different was merely gullible.

As for the Caswells, they were the lowest of the low, jackals feeding on grief, but now they had been caught in the act. As he stacked his copy and clipped it, he hoped they would be sent down for a long time.

He rose and stretched, feeling exhilarated. It was the best part of the job, clipping the copy, a good job done. He knew from experience that the elation did not last, a few hours at most until the anxiety set in about the next job, a few hours not to be wasted.

He reached for the phone and stabbed at the buttons. Melanie came on with a 'Yeh, what is it?'

'Lunch,' he said. 'I owe you one for putting you through all that grief.'

'Gimme ten minutes,' she said.

He dropped the phone back on the cradle, thinking about her. She was excellent to work with, tough as they came without losing an old-fashioned femininity. She hadn't been raised in the city and it still showed. Somewhere in Idaho, she'd told him. A small town, a Roman Catholic upbringing. Maybe, he thought, it was that ancient Catholicism which had caused her to flinch last night. She had certainly acted the part well but, if she had been scared, she hadn't let it affect her work.

'You can't get rid of the nuns and their teachings,' she had said once. 'Even if you discount it with your intellect, you can't purge it from your emotions.'

Even he, John Baxter, sceptic, could understand that.

'See, the story had a double impact,' the fat reporter was saying to a young female colleague. 'Not only did the woman say she had been given a quick flip round the galaxy in a flyin' fuckin' saucer, she had also been given the cure for cancer by the little green men. So, for a rag like ours, we had two major subjects in one story.'

He paused as Baxter and Melanie squeezed between them on their way to a table, nodded at them in recognition. They could hear his voice as they eased their way through the bar.

'We had the lot. Pictures of the woman with a State trooper, pointing at the circle of burnt grass where the thing had landed.' There was a pause as the woman asked a question. 'Yeh, sure, it was the South. Alabama or somewhere. It's always the South. So, I thought I had the story of the week until I put the question: how could you tell it was a flyin' saucer? And she said . . .' He paused for effect. 'She said, "Because it had UFO written on the side." '

Baxter groaned as he took his seat. He had heard the story dozens of times. He'd told it himself more than once. He could do without hearing it again. Melanie smiled at him.

'Something wrong?'

'Professional menopause,' he said. 'Think I've got a terminal case of déjà vu.'

'World weary, huh?'

'Yeh. Too many villains. Too many Caswells in this world. It gets to you in the end.'

A waiter appeared and plopped a card in front of them. His jacket was spattered in beer and soup but no one worried. The bar and grill on Forty-fourth and Second was excused everything. It catered for newspapermen and women and it survived through mutual tolerance. The management knew the problems of its clients and could rustle up burgers and booze to reporters at any hour. They understood the behaviour of the wilder ones and rarely went in for criticism the next day. No one would ever be barred from the place. You'd have to commit worse than murder. And they cashed cheques, night and day.

Baxter ordered a cheeseburger done medium and a lot of wine. Melanie a salad.

'Okay,' she said. 'You've got five minutes of sympathy and no more. Sympathy can be counterproductive you know.'

But he didn't need it. He knew what his problem was. He was simply getting too old for the job. His life was becoming repetitive and dull. His scepticism was souring into cynicism and it was time to do something else.

An hour and a jug of wine later he told her.

'I've made a decision. I'm going to buy the Amityville house . . .'

Her look of concern went unnoticed.

'You're serious? About *that* house?'

'Yep. If Nancy's lawyers leave me with the price of a roof over my head.'

Melanie knew all about the impending divorce, that it would be final in six weeks, and she felt ambivalent about it. She hoped Baxter would be happier on his own but she didn't like the idea of marital breakdown. It went against her upbringing.

Worse still, there was a child. Susan was sixteen, an age when the divorce of parents can be catastrophic. She asked how the girl was coping.

'Better,' he said. 'Kids are pretty resilient.'

The sadness in his voice made her want to mother him. She resisted the temptation.

Four o'clock and they were into the brandies and Melanie brought the house up again. She wanted to advise him against it, but she knew that the argument would not be rational.

'What do you need with a house anyway?' she asked brusquely.

'Have you seen my apartment?'

He knew very well that she hadn't. She had never been invited, but she'd heard that it was pretty impersonal, hard to take after the intimacy of a family home, and she knew that he still hadn't adjusted to living alone; it had been only a couple of months but he hadn't begun to handle it yet.

'You've never looked around,' she said weakly. 'You can do much better than that place.'

'Nope.' He shook his head vigorously. 'I could never do better. He's practically giving it away.'

'And why do you think that is?'

He smiled sweetly at her. 'Because people are so damn superstitious.'

She shook her head, wanting to tell him that he was crazy, but she knew it would be hopeless. What could she say? The house is haunted? It makes me feel cold and uncomfortable? He would simply laugh and make her feel like a silly emotional teenager. So she changed the subject.

Half an hour later she insisted that she had to get back and check her prints.

'Next time's on me,' she said.

'You bet.' He had decided to stay on for another one at the bar. It was Friday, the magazine was being put to bed, and his friends were relaxing, some of them relaxing spectacularly. He would stay for one drink, he thought. He watched Melanie admiringly as she left. If she weren't a colleague . . . He smiled to himself and headed for the bar.

*

A young printer was waiting for her in the darkroom, a keen lad, always willing to help, and Melanie had come to rely on him. Until they had met, she had always preferred doing her own developing but he was so keen, and so good at it, she occasionally allowed him to work on her pictures. But that afternoon he looked worried, as if he had fouled up.

At first she could see nothing wrong. The prints were hanging on pegs, ten-by-eights of the seance and they looked good, better than they had any right to look in the circumstances. She especially liked the look of hatred on Emma's face and was reminded of the obscene spitting.

'It's these over here,' he said, leading her to a table. 'What film were you using this morning?' he asked.

'The usual. Why?'

He indicated a set of prints of Sanders in the basement, perfect in dctail, cxccpt for a blotch around his face, a fault in the printing, his face obscured by a filmy cloud of white. For an instant she panicked, thinking she was in trouble, until she remembered Baxter telling her that Sanders wasn't part of the story; so it didn't matter.

The young printer was upset. 'It's not my fault,' he said. 'Honest. It doesn't make sense.'

She looked at all the prints. No matter what part of the frame Sanders's face appeared in, it was obscured by the fault. As the boy said, it didn't make sense.

Now he was leaning over a developing tray, pulling another print out and holding it up to the light. It was a shot of Sanders and Baxter by the boathouse. Baxter was in sharp focus, but Sanders was a blur. But now the misty fault covered him completely, leaving just a faint ghost-like shadow.

A.3-D.—3

'And they're all the same,' said the printer. 'Weird, huh?'

Melanie felt cold again. The gooseflesh had risen on her arms and legs. Despite the brandies, she shivered. Like the lad said, it was weird. More than that, it was scary.

FOUR

Baxter awoke slowly and reluctantly, cursing himself and cursing his old friend who had suggested one for the road. It had been one too many, tipped the delicate balance of common sense. They had gone on to an Irish bar, then what? Memory blanks. It wasn't often that he drank too much but when he did he went out of control. Now there was the hangover to contend with. He stumbled to the fridge, grunted obscenities and poured himself a jug of orange juice, sat down and began to resurrect his memory.

He'd phoned Sanders to confirm the deal. That was okay. The decision had been made. Then he'd phoned Nancy. That wasn't okay. He remembered the accusing tone: you've-been-drinking, delivered with pursed lips. Then the next decision, helped by Dutch courage, to leave the magazine, at least for a six-month period, a sabbatical during which he was going to write his book. He'd told Harry in the Irish bar, which was okay. Telling Harry meant that he couldn't go back on it.

He glanced at his watch. He had slept late. With a busy day ahead he was already behind schedule. He gulped the orange juice and felt sick, but he had no time to be sick; there was no time for self-pity. He had to drag himself across the river to Long Island.

He arrived at midday at the house in Hempstead where he had lived for ten years; half his adult life, and now he felt sad that he and Nancy had failed. It was a waste; inevitable, perhaps, that they had married so young and naive; inevitable, perhaps, but sad none the less.

Nancy was out. He went to his study and the feeling of sadness intensified. She had done as he had asked and brought two tea chests from the attic into his study. They squatted by his desk, square and ugly, waiting to be filled with his books. Briefly he thought that maybe he could give the marriage one last try, but the moment passed as quickly as it had arrived. It was far too late for that. There was too much bitterness.

He cleared the top shelf first: European and American history, then politics. They filled the first case. The hardback novels filled the second. Again he glanced at his watch. He was going to have to hurry if he wasn't going to be late for Sanders. Baxter smiled to himself. The fat man was so keen on the sale that he had agreed to let Baxter move in immediately, rent-free while the surveys and searches were made and the contracts drawn up. It was ideal. If you were going to make a fresh start in life, there was no point in hanging around.

He was heaving the first case to the door when he heard Nancy's car draw up.

She stood for a moment in the doorway staring at him, a cold, clipped 'hello', making him feel like a burglar. She'd had her hair tinted auburn and she looked good, younger than thirty-eight, slim and fit-looking, a walking advert for her health club. It was just a shame that her expression didn't match.

'So, what's this house like?' The question was delivered formally, without curiosity.

'There's lots of room,' he said. 'Fresh air. Trees. The

house is a real Long Island antique. It's wonderful. I'll have a place to really work for the first time in my life.'

'I know. All you need is some room. All you need is peace and quiet.' The sarcasm corrupted the words. 'Well then, now you'll have it.'

'That's right.'

He didn't rise to the bait but he couldn't forget those arguments, when he had said exactly those words. The need for some peace and quiet. The marriage had gone sour because they had become irritated with each other. Terminally. There was no other woman. Nor, as far as he knew, was there another man. They had simply become annoyed with one another.

'You'll be able to work undisturbed, concentrate, get started on the Great American Novel.' Again the sarcasm, cutting deep, going for the jugular. It was nasty of her. He had opened up his soul to her about his need to write something real and now she was throwing the words back, contaminated, into his face.

'Come on, Nancy,' he said quietly. 'Don't make this tougher than it has to be.'

His passivity softened her. He wasn't fighting back and her bitterness began to evaporate.

'I have to admit,' she said, 'it saddens me to see you taking your things away.'

'Me too.'

They had moved outside. Baxter shoved the packing case into the back of the car and went back for the second one. Nancy followed him into his study, cursing the tears that clouded her vision.

'Before, the word divoce was something abstract, a legal term. Now it's real.'

For a moment Baxter was tempted to take her in his arms, but he fought the temptation. It would have been a cruel thing to do, delaying the inevitable. He picked up the second case, couldn't look at her.

'We made the right decision, Nancy. Neither of us was happy. I spent ten years of my life working for that lousy magazine so that you and Susan could have . . .'

'I never asked you for anything except necessities,' she said interrupting him, the bitterness back again.

A door slammed, killing the conversation. They turned as they heard the sound of voices, then a girl appeared in the doorway.

Baxter called to his daughter and she ran into his arms. If he had achieved nothing else in life, this young woman made everything worthwhile. Susan was his success story. She was tall like her mother, still carrying a layer of puppy fat, bright faced with no need for make up. The traditional problems of adolescence had so far passed her by. She was bright, funny, clever and pulsing with common sense. He couldn't fault her.

She kissed him, said she didn't know he was coming over.

'Here I am,' he said, they hugged each other once more. There had been tears for weeks when the divorce was first mentioned but now she was making the best of it, even joking about having two houses. He ruffled her hair and glanced over her shoulder as a movement in the doorway distracted him.

'Hello, Mister Baxter.' Lisa was three months older than Susan and they had been best friends for ten years. The 'hello' was delivered in a husky whisper, eyelashes fluttering, posing in profile against the door. Lisa was at the stage of testing out her sexuality on men. Baxter smiled, finding her flirtation amusing and unwilling to admit to himself that it was more than slightly disturbing. It had been a long time since he had been with a woman, and here was a girl who was young enough to be his daughter. His smile widened at the cliché and he stepped forward to shake her hand.

'I hear you're buying yourself a haunted house,' she said.

News travelled fast. It was only last night that he had called Nancy.

'I'm only buying the house,' he said. 'Not the ghosts.'

Susan grabbed his arm. 'Can we come and see it, Daddy? It's not all that far is it?'

'Sure. Come any time you want.' She obviously didn't remember the stories. She would only have been a kid when the murders had been committed.

He looked around, at Susan's adoration, at Lisa's youthful seductiveness. It would have been an idyllic setting, were it not for Nancy's scowl of disapproval. His wife wanted him to go and she was right. He no longer belonged in this house . . .

Sanders was singing as he drove into Amityville. 'What a difference a day makes,' he warbled. He could not believe his luck. Okay, it would be a loss, but at least the damned house would be off his hands and he could forget about it. The Caswells had done him a favour after all, by finding him a buyer. He was a happy man. He wasn't even perspiring. Last night he had surprised his wife by making love to her. She couldn't believe it. He felt ten years younger. As soon as the house in Ocean Avenue was off his hands, then business would surely improve. It had been an albatross round his neck. A white elephant crossed with an albatross; that was 112 Ocean Avenue; a clapboard monster. He had felt ill since the day he had bought it;

one damn head cold after another. Now perhaps he could get on with his life in peace.

He pulled into the drive and stopped the station wagon in a spray of gravel. Baxter's car wasn't to be seen and briefly he felt a tremor of panic. Maybe the man had changed his mind. He checked his watch. No, there was still time. He wouldn't be long.

He fished in his pocket for the key and let himself in, crossed the hall to the living room and yawned, then jumped, startled at the sound of floorboards creaking. Someone was moving around in one of the bedrooms.

He shouted Baxter's name. Must have come in a cab, he thought.

'It's Sanders. I'm here.'

No reply. He felt himself shiver again, the same cold clammy perspiration, and, as he climbed the stairs, he was aware once again of the thumping of his heart.

He reached the first floor landing and cocked his head, bird-like, listening. The doors were shut. He reached for the door of the master bedroom and stopped as he heard the boards creak again above him in the attic. What was Baxter playing at, wandering around, not answering him?

He ambled across to the stairs. The bathroom door was ajar but he didn't look in, didn't see the mirror by the basin frost over as he passed. He shivered, rubbed his hands together, wondering where the sudden chill had come from in the height of summer. The stairs groaned under his weight and he cursed his obesity. Baxter hadn't made the stairs creak. He had gone up in silence.

By the time he had reached the top landing he was out of breath, one podgy hand on his chest, as if holding his heart in. He was angry, wondering why Baxter was playing games with him. He could hear him in the playroom, the room with the half-moon windows. As he reached for the doorknob, it turned and the door was pulled open.

Sanders fixed a smile, puffed into the room, hand outstretched. 'Mr Baxter.' The greeting died. The room was empty. He turned, thinking the man must be behind the door. It slammed shut of its own accord. He was alone.

'Oh, Jesus.'

At first the sound was low, just a hint of a noise, a soft buzz like a power drill in the distance. Sanders frowned, wondering where it came from. Steadily it grew in intensity. He looked at each wall, thinking of Caswell, wondering where the little bastard had hidden the speakers this time. He thumped a wall. Could they have been built in behind the plaster? The noise had increased now to the level of pain, a grating buzz like a thousand hacksaws, punctuated by intermittent squeals, like chalk screeching against a blackboard. He clamped his hands over his ears but the noise only grew. He ran to the door and pulled at the knob but it would not turn. It was a nightmare. He shut his eyes and told himself that when he opened them, the noise would have stopped and he would calmly walk out of the room and down the stairs and out.

He counted to ten, opened his eyes and saw a mass of flies, dozens of them, maybe hundreds in a swarm by the window and he remembered one of the previous owners saying that she had seen flies in winter, hundreds of them. He hadn't believed the stories of course. It was all part of a hoax, or at best a hallucination.

He gazed, stupefied, at the swarm wondering how it had got in. The window was closed. There was no chimney. He tried to think, to make some sort of sense but the noise had ripped something apart in his brain and he could make sense of nothing.

And now the flies were increasing in number, the swarm bulging and pulsing, thousands of tiny black bodies in an orgy of copulation. Again he tried to pull at the door but his hand wouldn't obey. He stood motionless. He couldn't feel his legs. There was a terrible pain in his chest and left arm and he could hear his heartbeat, pulsing in rhythm with the swarm.

'Please God,' he shouted but his voice was lost in the cacophony. At last he could move his arm. He tugged at the knob but it was jammed. He tried to kick at the door but his foot barely made contact.

'Oh, Christ,' he grunted, and as his lips parted, a fly zipped into his mouth.

He spat in disgust, clawing the remains from his tongue, then stared at his fingers. Flies were crawling over them. He flapped his hands to get rid of them and caught another insect in his eye. He wiped it away, aware of the broken body smearing itself across his eyeball. Again he swore and wished he had kept his mouth shut as the flies bombarded his lips. He spat, clawed flies from his nostrils and covered his face with his arms, but he could not escape them. They were everywhere. Involuntarily he opened his eyes and saw only a throbbing blackness. It was like being inside a blackcurrant.

Now they were in his ears, blocking out the noise and all he could hear were the insects burrowing deeper, towards his brain. He tried to prise them out but the movement of his fingers left his mouth and nose unprotected. He clenched his teeth but they squirmed inside, dying in their dozens but even as he spat out the filth, another squadron attacked.

He was choking in flies. He tripped and fell and they covered him. A second black skin. Moaning deep in his throat, clawing at his face, he thrashed on the floor, twisting and turning his great bulk, trying to crush them, but for every thousand killed, more attacked him until the whole room was a mass of black.

He screamed silently, called out for help, prayed to Jesus, the saviour of his childhood and as he shrieked out the name of Christ, a kamikaze swarm of flies filled up his throat and soiled his lungs. And still he fought them, until there was no more breath in him and he lay twitching, covered in a black pulsing shroud.

Baxter hated being late. To him, punctuality was a supreme virtue. It was part of the job. Arrive late on a story and you'd find that the opposition had got away with it. A friend had lost his job once because he had missed a plane. His excuse that the roads to the airport were jammed had cut no ice with his boss. He should have known. What were radios for if not to tell you about goddamn traffic jams.

As he reached Amityville, he realized he could forget about deadlines for a while. Maybe it wouldn't be the Great American Novel, as Nancy had said sneering at him, but it would be something between hard covers with his name on it. He'd never seen his name in print. *Witness* reporters were anonymous, a practice which made a lot of sense. It was just that he wanted to see his name on something for once.

He pulled up next to the station wagon and noticed that the door of the house was open. He checked his watch, cursed and ran inside, shouting Sanders's name. There was no reply. He tried the boathouse, came back, looked in the basement, then made for the stairs.

'Sanders!' he roared.

The response was a strangulated wheeze, coming from the attic.

He ran up the two flights. Just as he reached the top, he stumbled, gasping in shock as a fat arm swung through the banisters, the podgy fingers twitching. He grabbed at the rail to stop himself falling and leapt up the remaining stairs. Sanders was lying on his belly, eyes like pebbles, staring sightlessly at the wall, his tongue protruding, blue and swollen. Baxter groaned. He had seen many dead men and each time he prayed he would never see another.

He bent and touched Sanders's shoulder. The man grunted and the body shuddered at his touch, a last fluttering of life, then he lay still, on his stomach. There was one final indignity to come. As Baxter moved the body on to its back, Sanders broke wind, long and loud, and Baxter turned away in reluctant disgust. He felt the bile rise in his throat and he hoped that he would make the bathroom in time.

Melanie arrived as the body was being lifted into the ambulance. For a moment she panicked, until one of the ambulancemen told her that John Baxter was okay. He was in the house somewhere. She ran inside, calling his name. From the kitchen came the sound of running water. She pushed open the door and saw Baxter leaning over the sink washing his face.

'John, what on earth . . . ?'

He turned, his face white with nausea. 'Sanders. A heart attack. Or a stroke or something. I don't know . . .'

She put her arms round him and hugged him, looked over his shoulder searching for something. Then she saw what she was looking for. The brandy bottle was unopened. She picked it up and reached for a glass, thought better of it and picked up two glasses.

An hour later Baxter was composed enough for Melanie to show him the reason for her visit. She took a set of prints out of a yellow jiffy bag and spread them on the kitchen table. At first Baxter didn't get the point. He was looking at himself; the narcissus streak, interested in how he came across, worrying about his paunch. Melanie had to point out the fault in the film.

'Odd,' he said. 'Something wrong with the film?' Baxter knew nothing about photography. He was the type who stuck a thumb in front of the lens when taking holiday snaps.

'Just those particular frames?' said Melanie, talking to him as if to a child. 'Just those areas of the frames where Sanders happens to be? Come on, John . . .'

'So, what do you want me to say?' He was genuinely puzzled, by the pictures and by her nervousness.

'I don't want you to say anything. Just acknowledge to me that something is very strange here.'

Baxter shrugged. He didn't know what she was talking about.

'I'll spell it out,' she said. 'The day after these were taken, Sanders snuffs it.'

'So?' said Baxter. 'He was a sick man. You saw him. A ready-made candidate for intensive care if ever there was one. That fat bloated sweating face. He's the sort of guy that would order an ambulance after a meal rather than a taxi.'

Melanie ignored the flippancy. 'So you don't find all this . . .' she tapped one of the prints, 'a startling coincidence?'

'That's exactly what I find it. Nothing more.'

'Okay. Fine.' Tightlipped, she began to gather the photos together and stuffed them into the bag. For an instant, Baxter was reminded of his wife.

'Melanie, don't you see what you're doing? You're demonstrating exactly how superstition works.'

'I know, I know. I'm just an irrational female. Don't mind me. I'll probably go hysterical in a minute.'

The sarcasm, thought Baxter. Just like Nancy. He placed his hands on her shoulders and smiled.

'I don't mean that,' he said, 'and you know it. I appreciate what you're trying to say but it's all academic anyway. I'm still going to live here despite you trying to scare me off.'

She blinked, opened her mouth, then twitched, startled at the sound of a motor horn. Baxter turned and looked out of the window to see a truck drawing up in the drive.

'My stuff's arrived already,' he said. 'Stick around and help me. All the wine you can drink.'

Melanie conceded. She would help him with his furniture. She would drink his wine, but she would not forget about the photographs; nor would she let him forget. She would nag him until he saw reason, or whatever passed for reason.

FIVE

It was a bright morning. The only cloud was on the face of Nancy Baxter as she watched her daughter climb into her husband's car. She oozed anxiety.

'Fasten your seatbelt, Susan.'

The girl did as she was told, waved goodbye.

'Six o'clock now,' Nancy said. 'I mean it.'

Susan haggled for time. 'What if it's seven?'

'Six.' The word hissed out of her like venom.

Baxter switched on the ignition. 'Six it is,' he said. So petty, he thought. What difference would an hour make? But he would not argue. He had long since vowed that Susan would not become the rope in their marital tug-of-war, and so he had agreed to all of Nancy's demands, big or small, justified or not. The result was that Susan had become even closer to him. She recognized what he was doing, why he kept turning the other cheek. It was done for her sake and she loved him all the more for that.

The car moved away along the avenue. In his driving mirror he could see her, standing at the gate, a lonely figure, watching. She did not wave.

They arrived at midday. It was hot, the bare trees incongruous by the river bank. Susan whooped with delight when she saw the house and was out of the car before it had come to a halt. She ran round it, skipping like a foal, then ran to the pool and on to the boathouse. Baxter opened the door and watched her, felt a mixture of emotions, an intense love for her, mingling with sadness that he would see only fifty per cent of her development. He was going to miss that fifty per cent very badly and he had vowed to make the most of the time he had with her.

She followed him into the living room, ooh-ing and ah-ing, touching the furniture, the couch from his old study, the leather armchair, the prints and photographs scattered on the floor.

'I like it.'

'Thank God,' he said in mock relief. He took her hand. 'We'll start at the top.'

He told her his plans for it, what paint he was going to buy, where he was going to hang his pictures. As they reached the top landing, he had a flash of memory, of Sanders lying dying, and he shivered. A pang of nausea shot through him and he had to grab the banister as he had done the day before to stop himself falling.

Susan had rushed ahead and pushed open the playroom door. It had not been touched. It was bare and bleak. Old boards creaked as she walked to the open window, her hair fluttering in the breeze. She shivered, rubbed her arms and shut the window, slamming it down hard, too hard, so that the pane rattled.

'Oops,' she grimaced an apology at her father. It wouldn't do to go around breaking windows; hardly a good beginning.

'Sure you haven't seen a ghost yet?' she asked.

'Not yet.' He looked closely at her. 'Did you read the piece?'

She nodded and blushed; it was something of a confession. Young women weren't supposed to read things like *Witness Magazine*. It was a situation that Baxter had had to learn to live with, working for a magazine he wouldn't want his daughter to read.

'Lisa had a copy,' she said, by way of mitigation.

Baxter nodded. Lisa *would* have a copy. Lisa was the kind that kept the magazine's circulation healthy.

'Just for the record,' he said, 'not only have I never seen a ghost, I have never met anyone who claimed to see one who would last twenty seconds with a lie detector.'

'How can you be so sure?'

Baxter sighed and went into a well-worn routine. 'Experience,' he said. '*Witness Magazine*'s had me in more haunted houses and seances and psychic confrontations than I can tell you about. And you know what? They've all had one thing in common, a unity of theme.' He paused, tapped her lightly on the tip of her nose. 'It's all about the exploitation of the fear of death.'

'But isn't it natural to fear death?' she said, missing the point. 'Isn't it natural to wonder what's beyond death?'

'It's the most natural thing in the world. But there are no answers. Rationality doesn't apply. And people like the Caswells make use of that fear. They prey on it. It's the grossest form of immorality I know.'

He could hear himself preach and he smiled sadly at her. 'Not that I'm any paragon of virtue. I've been working for *Witness*. I'm in there, exploiting away with the best of them.'

She grasped his hand, recognizing his dilemma, tried to comfort him.

'But that's not the same thing, Daddy.'

'That's what I've been trying to tell myself. Anyway,' he spun on his heel, spread his arms to the ceiling, 'I find it ironic that this house, this monument to paranoia and fraudulent fear, has become the catalyst for my new, quote, serious, unquote life.'

'You're going to write your book here?'

'I'm sure going to try.'

He smiled and led her to the door. 'Time to move on, ma'am. Lots more to see.'

Hand in hand they moved downstairs, comfortable in each other's company. Baxter was looking forward to writing the book. It would give him self-respect. More than that, it would secure the respect of Susan. At present she didn't mind that he had made a living out of *Witness*, but maybe when she was older she would wonder and he could not bear the possibility that she might begin to despise him. He had the love of a girl, but he would need the respect of the woman.

SIX

Elliot West was delighted to receive a call from Melanie. Of course he would see her. Of course she could come to his office that day. No, he wasn't too busy. When he put the phone down, he playfully scolded himself. Anyone but Melanie would have had to make an appointment. He was a busy man with a full work schedule but for this woman he was prepared to drop everything. It was very unprofessional, but he had always been a sucker for a pretty face.

West was thirty-nine and had been widowed for two years. Now he was ready for someone new and exciting in his life. He had watched Melanie closely after the seance. She had been scared but she had fought hard to conceal it; an attractive, intelligent woman with a trace of vulnerability. It was a seductive combination and he was in no mood to fight it.

It would be good to see her on this territory where he would be relaxed and in charge. He glanced round his office. It was a spartan room, just a desk, two chairs and filing cabinets. Sometimes the people who came to see him were disappointed that it didn't contain computers and esoteric scientific instruments and, if he felt like showing off, he would take them to the lab and show them round, explaining the function of a thermo camera, or a spectrophoto fluorometer, taking an adolescent delight in their bemused fascination.

Melanie, he noticed immediately, was not to be one of these. She hardly bothered looking round, just sat down and smiled nervously at him. She was under stress and trying to hide it, but West could spot it. He was, after all, something of an expert on stress.

She wasted no time in coming to the point, laying a set of prints on his desk. He flipped through them, then examined them in detail through a magnifying glass. His first automatic thought was of the hoaxes that had been perpetrated over the years, the so-called examples of ectoplasm emanating from mediums, spirits called up and appearing in milky form.

Melanie was looking at him, wanting to be reassured but it was too early for that.

'I don't know what to say at the moment,' he said. 'You're sure the camera was working properly.'

'It was.' Christ, she thought, it's obvious the damned camera was working properly. How could a fault follow a man around? Surely West, of all people, could see that. Maybe there was an excuse for Baxter. He was, after all a professional sceptic and well known for stubbornness, but she expected better of West.

'Okay,' he said. 'What I can do is send these down to lab, the negatives, paper, camera, the lot. You've brought the camera?'

Melanie nodded.

'If there's a physical explanation,' West said, 'we'll find it.'

'And if there isn't?'

'Let's wait and see.' He gave her his professional, bedside-manner smile. It didn't work.

'You've seen the pictures,' she said, 'and you know what happened to Sanders . . .'

'I know, I know,' he said, interrupting her. 'It seems

fantastic, a convergence of events that can only be supernatural, but let me tell you that almost every day of the week we get something in here, some phenomenon, some situation that seems to be every bit as strange as your photos. I start off being baffled. It's an occupational hazard, then we find the reason. Most of the time it's so obvious you wonder why it wasn't spotted immediately.'

She stared at him, looking vulnerable again, wanting to believe him. She was one of the reluctant ones, wanting to be told that everything was explicable, wanting him to rub out the doubt.

'In ninety-seven per cent of the cases,' he added, 'there turns out to be a perfectly logical explanation.'

'And the other three per cent?'

He smiled. 'The other three per cent is why I'm here.'

She nodded and got to her feet, took the camera from her bag and handed it over, thanked him and left.

Baxter shut the door of the Clifton Sloane Agency office behind him and made his way quickly towards the lift. The literary agent had encouraged him to write his book and he had stayed too long. He was in danger of being late for Melanie, who was due at the house by six. He'd taken the precaution of telling Dolores, his new cleaning lady, that Melanie would be arriving, but he didn't want to leave her alone in the house. Her fears were unfounded but her nervousness was real enough.

He drummed his fingers impatiently against the wall as he watched the floor indicator. It was an old building and an antediluvian lift.

Slowly it climbed towards him, then stopped at floor 14.

'Come on, come on,' he grumbled. Briefly he thought of running down the stairs but seventeen floors was a long way.

Then it was moving again and he could hear it wheeze up the shaft, like an old man panting up a staircase.

16

17

The doors creaked open and he stepped into a tin box with a wrought-iron grille for a ceiling. One thing about Sloane, he thought; he couldn't be accused of being ostentatious. He wasn't the Four Seasons and Polo Lounge type.

He tapped the Ground floor button and sighed as the lift slowly made its descent.

17

16

15

Without warning it lurched to a halt, throwing him off balance so that he stumbled against the back wall. He swore and banged the button again. The lift had stopped between floors and he shivered, feeling claustrophobic. He had always had a fear of confined spaces, ever since he was a kid, an irrational phobia he thought he had conquered, but now it crept back at him.

There was no movement. He glanced at his watch again and stabbed at the red emergency button. Somewhere in the bowels of the building he could hear the trilling of an alarm bell, but the lift did not move. He tried to shout but his mouth was dry. His throat seemed to have closed up. At first he didn't notice the fly on the grille or pay any attention to the buzzing. It flew up into the shaft, circling it, then darted back into the lift and settled above his head against the wall.

He tried to whistle but his mouth was too dry. When he yelled, his voice was no more than a grunt. The fly caught his eye and he looked at it without interest, then glanced up through the grille at the cables that stretched up through the blackness of the shaft to the roof, twenty floors away. He was trapped about half way up the shaft, annoyed, frustrated and helpless.

Damn it, he grunted, thinking about Melanie waiting for him at the house. Maybe Dolores would stay with her until he arrived. It not, she would leave. Damn this goddamn tin can to hell.

The cables tensed and creaked and the lift lurched once more and began to move up the shaft, slowly at first then suddenly fast as if some enormous force were dragging it towards the roof. Baxter slipped and fell, stared wide-eyed at the indicator. It was no longer an old man wheezing upwards. It had turned into an express litt, heading for the roof like a rocket out of Canaveral.

Baxter yelled in fear, unable to take his eyes off the indicator, the figures chasing one another until they became a blur.

25, 26, 27 . . .

. . . another couple of floors and it would be P for Penthouse. He screamed, thinking back to his days as a young reporter when he had covered a story of a lift crashing. The cables had snapped. He remembered the autopsy report, four people flattened like toads under a truck, their spines impacted.

With a snap of the cables, the lift stopped dead, throwing Baxter into the door, skinning his elbows and knees. The indicator registered the fact that he was stuck again between the twenty-ninth floor and the roof. He scrambled to his feet and pushed the Penthouse button. The hell with it, he thought. I'll get out at the top and walk down, no matter how long it takes.

There was no movement. He yelled for help and his voice came back as an echo from the depths of the shaft. The alarm bell was still ringing, weaker now, like a kid's bicycle bell, over two thousand feet below.

Maybe, he thought, if he could open the grille, he might be able to climb on to the top of the cage and push open the door to the penthouse. It was worth a try.

He remembered just twenty minutes ago, standing on the pavement looking up at the building. Thirty storeys didn't look much, compared with some of the buildings in Manhattan, but from the top it was a hell of a way down and he remembered the old theory that the people who threw themselves off scrapers were dead before they hit the ground.

'Oh God,' he said aloud. 'They'd need to shovel me up.' He'd be nothing more than a greasy spot, another impacted spine.

He had to do something. He balanced his brief case on its end against the door, then stepped on it, and reached for the grille. It was held in place by four screws. He stuck his thumbnail into the first and twisted. The nail broke and he grunted in pain.

The fly on the wall seemed to be watching him, no more than a few inches from his face. He glanced at it and felt a chill pass through him. The fly began to move, spinning in slow circles and it seemed to Baxter that it sparkled, as if covered in sugar. He turned and ignored it, shoved his other thumbnail into the screw and twisted. It began to move. Suddenly the fly buzzed into his face. He slapped at it, back-handed, his foot slipping on the briefcase, sending him falling back into the set of buttons, crashing into them, hitting all 31 of them as he fell.

The lift shuddered and dropped down the shaft, fast, as if nothing were holding it, as if the cables had snapped. Again the indicator spun and Baxter was thrown face first against the wall, pinned like a butterfly, the force of the descent glueing him to the aluminium.

He could feel a scream build in his throat, then it was smothered as the force of the descent sucked the breath from his lungs. His face was pressed against the wall, and all he could see, glancing to one side was the box containing the emergency phone. In his panic, he had not noticed it before. Now, as the car plummeted into the blackness, the box was forced open and the receiver shot into the air, suspended by its cord, seeming to defy the laws of gravity, the instrument fluttering in the draught, just out of his reach, while behind him, the indicator spun . . . 15, 14, 13, 12, in a blur of yellow, and Baxter's body shuddered and he thought what a stupid, meaningless way to die . . .

SEVEN

Melanie groaned as she pulled up outside the house. Baxter's car was not there. She had assumed that he would have arrived before she did. She had even driven slowly in order to be ten minutes late; and he knew that she was nervous about the house. She got out and reached for her coat, slung it over her shoulders. It was cold for the time of year, the setting sun giving hardly any heat.

She'd noticed too that, as she had reached the drive, the lights were on in the attic, the shades half drawn against the half-moon windows, so that the house seemed to be winking at her. She'd retaliated by sticking her tongue out at it. Now she saw that the front door was open. She climbed the steps and waited, uncertain whether to go in. She couldn't remember the name of John's cleaning lady. Quickly she fished in her handbag for her notepad and looked it up. Dolores. She was dreadful with names, could never fit them to faces.

She pushed the doorbell but there was no answering sound and so she shoved the door wider. It swung with a squeak of old hinges needing to be oiled.

'Hello? Dolores?'

No reply. She glanced round the hall and into the living room, feeling clammy. It always seemed to be cold in the house. She felt uncomfortable, both physically and mentally, but she wasn't going to let the place get to her. She decided that she would wait in the living room, settle down with a book until he arrived, anything to take her mind off the place. She took two paces and froze as she heard footsteps in one of the upstairs rooms.

'Dolores?' she shouted. Still no reply. She turned and made for the stairs, slowly took the first two and stopped, listening. You were so defenceless on stairs, wandering up, looking at nothing. Anyone or anything could launch itself at you from the landing and . . . she told herself to stop imagining things. This was the stuff of comics, the fear of nothing at all. She was a grown woman. She'd been half-way round the world in her job. She was far too mature to be scared by creaking floorboards.

They creaked again and she turned and ran for the door, thinking only of getting out, running single-mindedly across the hall to the open door. It had slammed shut. She grabbed the handle and pulled. It was stuck. It would turn neither right nor left and she had a flash of memory, of the window in the sewing room. And now she knew that she hadn't closed it the other day. The footsteps were louder now, crossing the landing towards the stairs. She did not dare look. She simply turned and ran, moving fast, not knowing where she was going, running blind, away from the sound that grew louder with each step.

In the living room, the windows were shut tightly. She couldn't budge the latches. She spun around. The door to the basement was open and she thought of going down but as soon as the idea arrived, she rejected it. She wasn't going down there. She would be trapped, like a rat. Better to get out the back somewhere even if it meant going through the hall again and confronting whatever it was that was coming down the stairs.

She tiptoed across the room to the door and cautiously peered round. There was no one to be seen. She tried to think. Where was the back door? She couldn't remember. Her brain seemed to be frozen. Taking a deep breath, she dashed towards the nearest door. It was closed, like everything else. The place was a prison. Whimpering like a puppy, she turned, sprinted down a corridor, running now without thought, praying for an open door. She hit a door with her shoulder and half fell into the kitchen. Something was standing there in the gloom, holding a club above its head, ready to strike.

Melanie screamed.

The creature screamed back at her.

They screamed at each other at full volume, a discordant screech of terror, both of them frozen in shock, screaming until there was no breath left. Then there was silence, except for the rasp of their breath.

Melanie's eyes grew quickly accustomed to the dark and she saw in front of her a large, fat woman, Hispanic, holding a torch above her head, looking as if she was going to faint.

'Dolores?' Her voice cracked in mid-syllable.

The woman nodded and lowered the torch.

'I'm Melanie.' The relief was almost edible. 'I'm here to see Mr Baxter.'

'He's not here.' The voice was high pitched, too small for such a big woman.

'I know,' said Melanie. 'I know . . .'

And still they trembled, for a full minute, until Dolores grinned and led Melanie towards the kitchen table, sat her down and poured her a cup of coffee.

Melanie felt a fool and her relief brought on a fit of giggles. Laughing at her irrational fears, two grown women acting like kids. The tension evaporated, Dolores began to talk.

The accent was hybrid, half Puerto Rican, half Brooklyn. She'd lived in Brooklyn for ten years and had been in Amityville only a few months and was glad to get a bit of extra work from Mr Baxter.

Sure, she said, she'd heard a lot of voodoo about this house but it hadn't bothered her, not until she'd heard Melanie running from room to room.

It was dark by the time Dolores was ready to leave. Melanie, watching her, began to feel another tremor of anxiety. She did not want to be alone again. She made an attempt to get her to stay a little longer but it was no good. The woman had a husband to go to and a meal to prepare, and besides, as she said, Mr Baxter would be here any minute.

Dolores collected her things, waved goodbye then stopped, tapped her temple and picked up the torch.

'You better have this,' she said. 'Fuses been going out all day. Electrical man couldn't come. You know where the fuse box is?'

Melanie nodded. It was in the basement. She remembered seeing it. Dolores grinned and left by the back door. No sooner had she closed it than Melanie shivered. She was cold again. She had not noticed it when she was talking to Dolores, but now she was clammy again. Drops of cold sweat ran down the inside of her arms. It was as if, by briefly opening the door, Dolores had let in a blast from the Arctic.

On an impulse she went to the back door and pulled it open, tried it a few times to make sure it wasn't stuck, like the front door. She decided to take the short walk to the boatyard. She'd seen some logs there, and kindling. She would make a fire. That's what she'd do. A fire in summer, but to hell with tradition. She was cold. When you're cold, Melanie, she told herself, you build a fire. Right? Right. Okay, let's go.

She was still talking to herself as she tried to light it, but the kindling wouldn't take. She went through a whole box of matches but achieved only a burnt thumb, and now it was getting colder by the minute. Permanent gooseflesh. The hell with it, she thought. If she couldn't get warm outside, she'd get warm inside.

She crossed the hall to the kitchen and began to rummage among the cupboards.

'Gotcha,' she said, pulling a bottle of brandy from a shelf. It was nearly full. She poured herself a shot and downed it in one, enjoying the fire in her throat and belly. She'd read somewhere that booze didn't raise body heat. It was only an illusion. Right then, she'd happily settle for the illusion, but the warmth did not last. Almost immediately she was shivering worse than ever.

Her coat lay on the floor of the hall where it had fallen when she ran from the sound of the footsteps. She slipped it on, feeling ridiculous, like an ancient crone, thin-blooded, shivering in summer. Where was the damned thermostat? She remembered seeing it somewhere. Then she spotted it at the end of the hall. Right, Melanie, she said aloud, let's blast this place fulla heat. She scuttled towards it, arms wrapped round her chest, her back bent as if she were heading into a gale.

She pulled one cold hand out from her armpit and touched the tiny dial. It read seventy.

'Crap,' she said aloud. 'Seventy, my ass,' then blinked at the sight of her breath, a light mist puffing out of her. With her thumbnail she nudged the lever along the grid. Seventy-five. Eighty. Eighty-five. There was a sharp tiny explosion, a flash of light and a small puff of blue smoke. And all the lights in the house went out.

Melanie cursed in the dark, long and loud. First no heating, now no light. Let there be light, she yelled. How the hell was John going to write his book in this damn freezing slum? It would drive him crazy. She waited until her eyes grew accustomed to the dark and went back to the kitchen. By now she was fatalistic. Probably no batteries in the flashlight, she told herself. She picked it up and snapped it on. The beam was bright. Thank God for small mercies.

Playing the beam ahead of her, she made for the basement door and pushed it open. She did not fancy the idea of going down there, then she began talking to herself again, saying she should pull herself together. What was she? Some sort of adolescent?

She went down the steps one by one, playing the torch around the walls, down towards the open well and up the back towards the fusebox. Holding it at arm's length she slowly made her way down, left foot forward, right leg dragging up to meet it, leaning against the banister for support. Something moved. She blinked, started, as a fly buzzed into the beam of light and hovered, as if caught in the beam.

Flies can't hover, she thought. They've got to keep on the move or else they drop. She'd never seen a fly hover before. It was physically impossible. As she looked at it, the beam began to fade, the light becoming yellow and cloudy. She turned it around and aimed it at herself. The lens was slowly frosting over.

She'd had enough. She scrambled back up the stairs. To hell with the fusebox. To hell with the house. She was getting out. Right now.

She burst into the living room and slammed the door behind her, leant against it, panting. Behind her she could hear the buzzing of the fly. It was an angry sound. She'd always hated clumsy figures of speech. Angry buzzing was silly and lazy. But in this case it was apt. The damned fly was good and mad.

She took a breath and pushed herself away from the door and, as she did so, it burst open and a blast of cold air hit her in the back, slamming her across the room and into the wall, the torch sweeping from her grasp and smashing against the wall.

She tried to get up but the wind was gale force. Fighting against it she managed to turn but she could not move forward. She could do nothing but stand there, arms and legs spread, starfish-like against the wall, watching as fingers of frost began to interlace on the window, unable to protect herself even as the frost began to form on her clothes, then on her arms and legs, her hands and her face. She screamed but her voice was a pitiful squeak, lost in the roar of the gale. Then her eyeballs began to ice up. She couldn't close her eyes. She could see the ice forming over the pupils, felt the nip of the frost, saw it happen, watched herself slowly going blind behind a thickening screen of ice, watching herself freeze into oblivion . . .

For the second time in twenty-four hours, Baxter pushed the car to its limit across Long Island. Maybe, as the maintenance man had said, he wasn't really fit to drive, but he had to get to the house. He was late; ages and ages. It had taken him nearly half an hour to recover.

What he remembered most clearly was the indignation on the man's face.

'I can't understand it,' he had said. 'It was inspected only last week,' as if it was Baxter's fault that the lift had plummeted almost thirty storeys, then slowly come to a stop half-way between the third and fourth floors. They'd pulled him out through the roof grille. All that was wrong was a few scratches and shock.

'The inspection certificate is right there in the car,' the man had yelled, pointing at it.

'Sure,' Baxter had said.

He glanced at his reflection. Some of his colour had returned but there were dark smudges beneath his eyes. Maybe he shouldn't be driving but he had to get to the house. He hadn't seen Melanie since early morning and he was worried about her.

He grunted with relief as he pulled into the drive and saw her car. At least she hadn't left. He ran to the door realizing immediately that something was wrong. The whole house was in pitch darkness.

'Melanie?' He hit the light switch and the chandelier burst into light. He blinked and crossed the hall, turned towards the living room and saw her, huddled on the floor in the far corner, her knees drawn up to her chin, arms wrapped round herself in the foetal position; and she was wearing a coat.

Again he called her name and turned on the living room lights. She blinked and sprang to her feet, flattened herself against the wall and slithered away from him, staring wide-eyed as if the sight of him terrified her.

'What happened?'

No answer. It was as if she had been struck dumb. Her body shuddered continually. Her lips trembled but she made no sound.

He reached out for her and without warning she swiped at him, back-handed, slapping at his outstretched arm, swatting him like an insect, shouting at him in a child-like voice to leave her alone.

Baxter blinked. He didn't understand. She scared him. He had been looking forward to her comforting him. He had his story all ready, about the lift that went berserk and nearly killed him. He was ready for a bath, a drink and some normal, friendly conversation; yet here was this terrified creature slapping at him. This wasn't Melanie. It looked like her but it couldn't be, not this creature with the voice of a child.

'For God's sake,' he yelled, backing off as she swung at him; then she was gone, side-stepping him like some football player, feinting left and running to his right, darting away and scampering to the hall.

He started moving too late. By the time he had run after her, she was in her car, turning the ignition and kicking it into gear. He yelled after her, pleading with her to wait and tell him what had happened, but she was gone in a spray of gravel, the car drifting out into the Avenue. He ran to the gate and stared after her. She was driving into the night, blind, with no lights. Again he yelled her name and was rewarded with a flash of her tail lights. At least that was something. She wasn't crazy enough to drive without lights in the dark. He watched the beam of her headlights turn north, then went back to the house, asking himself questions and getting no answers.

He would give her an hour, then ring her apartment. Maybe she would explain over the phone; and maybe not. She looked as though she had just seen a vision of hell.

EIGHT

Baxter had been away from the office for less than a week but already, as he walked through the corridors, it seemed like foreign territory. Everything looked the same, but he was aware of a subtle difference in the greetings of his ex-colleagues. He was no longer one of them. He was past tense and he thought he could detect a trace of resentment. Perhaps they were envious. After all, he was trying to do what most of them talked about. He was escaping the treadmill, working towards being his own boss. Or perhaps he was imagining it. He told himself to stop making things up. Less than a week of solitude and already he was showing the first signs of the writer's occupational hazard known as paranoia.

The picture editor told him that Melanie was down in the basement.

'Is she okay?' he asked.

'Surc. Why not? Whydya ask?'

Baxter shrugged.

'She's just had a few days off, that's all,' the man continued. 'Deserved it too.'

'Yeh,' said Baxter. The man was looking for a reason why he would ask if his photographer was okay, but what could he say? That he'd been trying for days to reach her, that she had hung up on him twice and when he went to her apartment, she wasn't there. That she hadn't answered a note he had left for her. That her answering service had said she was away and hadn't left a forwarding address or number. So what? Like the man said, she deserved a few days off.

He ran down to the basement, ignoring the lift. He'd had enough of lifts to last him a lifetime. He pushed open the door to the mole hole where the film was developed. The photographers called it the mole hole; blind moles working over their developing tanks.

At first the place seemed to be empty. The tanks were dry. Only a few prints were hanging from the lines. He looked past the tanks to a line of cubicles where the photographers worked on their prints. There was someone in the last cubicle, a silhouette, distorted by the frosted glass.

As he made his way towards her, he wondered how he would be received. Surely she would talk to him. She must have got over the shock by now, whatever it was.

For a moment he stood watching her. She had her back to him, wearing a T-shirt and jeans, He wanted to put his arms round her and protect her. If she'd let him.

'Hi.'

No response. She carried on working as if she had heard nothing.

'Melanie.' His tone was sharper now. This was ridiculous.

Still nothing.

'Look, this is crazy. Can we talk about it, whatever it is?'

'No.' Just a syllable. She did not even turn her head. Baxter felt a surge of annoyance. Why was she reacting like this?

'Well, I'm sorry,' he said. 'But I think you're going to have to talk about it.'

She turned, her face contorted with suppressed rage. But at what? What had he done? He stepped back as she jabbed her finger at him.

'Okay,' she said. 'The lights went out. Fuses or something. It was the most horrible thing that ever happened to me. The worst nightmare, the worst . . .' She stopped talking, blinked as if she were about to burst into tears, shivered and turned away from him again.

'I'll never go near that house again. Never.' The anger had left her and her voice was soft, like a child's.

He reached out for her, then drew his hand back. She had given no answer and he was confused. What did she mean about the lights? They were working when he found her. He told her so and immediately the anger flared in her again.

'I don't care if they worked for you,' she said, turning to him, the words spat at him. 'I don't want to hear about it, John. I don't want one of your so-called rational explanations. I know what I went through. I'm not crazy.'

Again he took a step back. He'd never suggested she was crazy. She was defending herself against a position that had never been under attack.

He fought to remain calm.

'Melanie, listen to me.' He hoped he was sounding firm without being patronizing. 'That house is enveloped in its own mystique. People expect things to happen there. So, things happen. That was the basis of the Caswells's operation . . .'

'Don't insult me, John,' she said, interrupting him,

the voice steadier now, the anger under control and all the more powerful for that.

'I'm not insulting you. I'm telling you something we both know to be true.'

She shook her head. 'I don't know what's true any more.' For a brief moment, he thought she was softening. He stepped towards her, held out his arms, but he had misread her mood. She slapped at his hand, the way she had done in the house. 'Now leave me alone. I've work to do.'

'No,' he said angrily. 'I won't leave it. Why do you think that whatever it was that happened, just happened to you? Why not to me too?'

'I don't know. Maybe the house has other plans for you.'

'Jesus,' he said. This was too much.

She turned away from him, bent over her work again.

'Get out of here, John. Please . . .'

There was nothing for him to do or say now. He backed off. You can't reason with someone who thinks that houses have wills of their own. He left the room and closed the door.

It was a thick door and he did not hear her begin to sob, nor could he knew that all she wanted in the world was for him to turn back and make her believe that everything was all right.

Susan Baxter was reluctant to admit the fact to herself but there was no getting away from it. Lisa had been getting on her nerves a lot lately. They had been friends for as long as she could remember, since the days when they looked after one another's dolls. They'd shared secrets and gone everywhere together. Now and again, as was natural, they squabbled, sometimes seriously, especially when Lisa tried to steal her boyfriends. The trouble was that she usually succeeded because she was prettier. Susan's puppy fat got in the way. In the early days, Nancy had seen what was happening and she had had a heart-to-heart talk, telling her that Lisa was basically insecure, that she needed to show off to Susan.

'Etcetera, etcetera,' Susan had said. Then, 'Don't you think that's pretty much first fuckin' grade psychology, Mom?' She had been thirteen at the time. It was the only occasion when she had sworn in front of her mother. She would never do it again. Couldn't bear to see the hurt expression on Nancy's face.

Still, taken all in all, they had been very close, Lisa and she, until the last six months, when Lisa had changed. Now she was smug and patronizing. The answer was obvious. She had done it with Jeff and now she felt double superior, a sixteen-year-old woman of the world. The problem was that now she was beginning to have other ideas. All this apparent interest in the Amityville house was a smokescreen. What the little bitch wanted was to flirt with Susan's father. Six months ago, it might have been dismissed by an old-fashioned word, like they used in 'fifties movies on TV. A 'crush'. Something like that. But now that Lisa had become a woman of the world, words like 'crush' had become redundant.

All week she had been pestering Susan to show her the house. When she asked why, Lisa would give one of her irritating little enigmatic smiles. Enigmatic was her flavour-of-the-month word. She used it all the time. It might have been more impressive, thought Susan, if she knew what it meant.

That morning, she had given in and taken the bus to Amityville. Anything to shut her up. Maybe, once she'd seen the house, she'd stop going on about it.

The bus dropped them half a mile from the house and by the time they had reached it, Susan was beginning to regret coming.

'Look,' she said, 'I don't think we should be here when Daddy's not home.'

'Why not? You've got your own key and everything.'

'I don't know. It doesn't seem right.

Lisa tutted, hands on hips, standing on the steps by the main door, and Susan knew that her friend held the better hand. She could have stood firm at home. There was no possibility of backing off now they were on the doorstep. Lisa added the clincher.

'What are you really afraid of?'

It was a dirty trick. Susan shook her head, pushed past Lisa and opened the door, shoved it hard and pushed her friend into the hall. For a moment they stood looking round. Susan was impressed. Her father had been busy. There were rugs on the floor and prints on the walls covering the bare patches. The house smelled fresh, a pine smell. The floorboards gleamed with varnish. It looked like a different house. Lisa made a little whoop of appreciation and ran into the living room, began making an inspection. Susan watched her from the doorway. The room was spotless. Her father had arranged one corner into a study. Typing paper was neatly stacked next to his typewriter. His favourite picture of her stood in a frame next to it. On the shelves between the books, stood three pictures of him as a younger man. Susan grinned as she saw Lisa inspect them.

'Did you know,' said Lisa, touching the back of her father's chair, 'that you can have sex with a ghost?'

'Really.'

'I've been reading about it. It's happened to a lot of women. They all say it's fantastic. What do you think?'

Susan shrugged. The idea was about as interesting to her as algebra.

Lisa came across and took her arm, leered at her. 'Maybe that's why your father bought the house. Huh? Maybe he's got some sex-starved ghost with enormous boobs in the attic.'

'Somehow,' said Susan with as much dignity as she could muster, 'that doesn't sound like my dad.'

Lisa merely grinned and made for the stairs. Again Susan followed, feeling a sudden accustomed chill. She rubbed her arms and tweaked her nose. She wished her father was with her. It wasn't the same without him. Lisa, running up the stairs, was still talking to her.

'I've read all your dad's articles, y'know. The whole story. I know all the details of what happened here.'

She affected what she thought was a sinister voice, low and slow, dragging out each syllable.

'Ron DeFeo murdered his father and mother, two sisters and brothers here . . .'

It should have sounded silly but Susan wished she'd stop. For some reason, Lisa was scaring her. She followed her into her father's bedroom, saw the big bed with the Indian rug on it, the smoked mirrors acting as a headboard. Lisa ran a hand along the bed and studied her reflection.

'This is where he began . . .' The same sepulchral tone; then she turned and pushed past Susan and crossed the hall to the adjoining doorway.

'Then here. He fired two more shots, the sound muffled by the crash of thunder outside.'

She leant back and gazed at the ceiling. 'Then he went upstairs to the children's rooms.'

She began to improvise her act, holding out her arms like a sleepwalker, moving past Susan and making for the attic. Susan followed, wondering why she couldn't dismiss Lisa's charade as the adolescent stupidity it was. Why was she allowing the little bitch to get to her?

Lisa turned at the top of the stairs and looked down at her with glazed eyes.

'Ron DeFeo, possessed by the spirit of the devil, in this house . . .'

'Cut it out, Lisa.' Susan surprised herself by the vehemence of her words, but she was sick of it. Lisa was being about as funny as a toothache.

'There is evil in this place,' Lisa moaned. But she couldn't maintain it. The actress suddenly became the giggling teenager, almost choking with laughter.

'Come on,' she said, when she had got her breath back. 'Let's go to the basement. There's a dry well there that's supposed to be the entrance to hell.' She ran past Susan who once more found herself following, grumbling to herself. For a sophisticated woman of the world, Lisa had no trouble regressing to the nursery.

In the basement Lisa went directly to the new planks which Baxter had placed over the well. He had not yet nailed them down and Lisa gleefully pulled one aside, peered into the void. Susan looked over her shoulder, reluctantly fascinated.

'It was burst open by some colossal supernatural power from the depths of the earth,' Lisa said, this time in her normal voice. She was enough of an actress to know when she had gone over the top. 'This is supposed to have been an ancient Indian burial ground. Their tortured spirits are still down there, waiting to rise up and reclaim their land.'

Susan had heard the stories. A chief of the Shinnecock had been buried, as was the custom, standing up. Around 1800 some boy had been digging a well and found the grave, stolen the skull and used it as a football. Ever since, there was said to be a curse on the place, the spirit of the chief taking his vengeance on anyone living in the house. She had read the stories and dismissed them as nonsense. But there was a small part of her that was scared. A piece of her soul still lived in the world of dreams where such things as beheaded Indians could still wreak vengeance.

But not Lisa. To her it was a joke, and now she was leaning into the well wailing like a banshee, the noise echoing, like the howl of an animal.

'Stop it, Lisa.' Again there was urgency in her voice.

Lisa caught the tone and turned, looking contemptuous. 'What's the matter? Afraid they'll answer back?'

She was about to reply when they heard a bang upstairs, the sound of a door slamming, followed by footsteps on the boards above. In that instant they became children again, gasping in fright, grabbing one another, huddling together, straining to listen. The footsteps approached the basement door and a shadow appeared on the stairs. Lisa moaned softly. Susan screamed, the scream dying in her throat as a face appeared, grinning down at them.

'Hi,' said Baxter.

Susan blew air like a whale. 'Oh, daddy,' she said. 'You scared us.'

'Scared you,' said Lisa, recovering her poise fast.

The first thing he wanted to know was why they were not at school. Another teachers' strike. He grimaced in disgust, wondering how his daughter would ever get her education. She was always off school. There were so many holidays, so many disruptions, it was a wonder she knew her alphabet. But he was glad to see her. Lisa had recovered her composure and was complimenting him on the house.

He found himself reacting to her flirtation and mentally slapped his wrist. There was a name for people like him. But there was no harm in it and he was glad to have them around.

The ritual of dishwashing was performed in silence. Nancy scrubbed at plates long after it was necessary, her face tight with annoyance. Susan stood next to her, taking each plate, cup, saucer, drying it absent-mindedly, sniffing back tears, fighting to remain composed in the face of her mother's surprise attack. They had been silent for fully three minutes now. Someone would have to give in and Susan had vowed that she would not be the one.

'I'm trying not to be unreasonable, Susan.' Nancy had finally decided to break silence. It was half-way towards an apology and Susan gratefully jumped at the chance.

'Mother, it was no big deal. Lisa's been bugging me to see the house. She's a complete fanatic about it, so we went up there. It was broad daylight. There was no danger. Daddy knew nothing about it until he came home.'

'I'm sure,' said Nancy sarcastically.

'He didn't.'

'I don't care whether he did or not. That's not the point.'

Nancy stopped herself. It was silly attacking Susan. The attack was misplaced. The girl had done nothing wrong. It was her own irrationality that had caused the outburst.

'It's the place itself,' she said weakly, knowing that she was now on the defensive.

'You haven't even seen it,' said Susan, pouting.

'I don't have to see it. I know all about it. Who doesn't? The place is infamous. Only a man with your father's colossal ego would consider living in it. I don't want you going near it. Is that understood?'

They glared at one another in silence.

'Is that understood?' she repeated.

'Yes.' A reluctant hiss, a result of a lifetime of doing as she was told, even when she considered the order to be stupid. Susan was no rebel. She loved her parents and recognized their problems, realized that sometimes she was the cause or the target of their anger. Sometimes, though, she thought that she, Susan Baxter, was just too damned good to be true.

Her reluctant obedience softened Nancy. She reached out and hugged her daughter and, when they broke apart, both were in tears.

'I'm afraid, Susan,' she admitted. 'It's as simple as that.'

Susan nodded. She knew what Nancy meant. There was something scary about the house. If it weren't for her father, she wouldn't go within five miles of it.

For twenty minutes Baxter had sat motionless, staring at a blank piece of paper protruding from his typewriter. Nothing was going to plan. The idea had been to show the two girls round the house, give them coffee, then take them back to Hempstead. Okay so far. It was the next part that was proving difficult. After dropping them off and making sure he didn't bump into Nancy, he would get back, pour himself a bourbon and finally make a start on Page One. He'd got back okay, poured the bourbon okay, put the goddamn ice in okay, but he hadn't written a line.

There had been nearly a week of this and he was close to despair. He had writer's block before he'd written a word. It was worse than his nightmares. He couldn't do it. He'd known it would be different from newspapers where you had facts and quotes and background, and it was a question of getting them all into a readable order, but this freedom of expression meant a net result of sweet nothing.

All week he had resisted the temptation to work out a detailed plot, in the belief that such a system would stifle spontaneity. The idea was to do a rough draft in the stream of consciousness style, write down the first thing that came into his head within the framework of the idea, then edit it into something comprehensible later. It was fine in theory. In practice, he had yet to type a lousy comma.

He'd cleaned the house while waiting for inspiration. He cleaned the oven. He whitened his tennis shoes. He'd done everything but write.

For the umpteenth time he rose from his chair and made a tour of the room. Everything was in order. He glanced along a line of books, praying for inspiration: Mailer, Dos Passos, Marquez, Graham Greene. They could do it. Why not John Baxter? He went back to the desk, picked up his glass and took a slug. Again everything was neatly arranged: the paper, the strips of correcting paper, thesaurus, dictionary. Another belt of booze. Maybe he should try it drunk. Maybe he should go for another walk. Maybe he should chuck the whole thing in and open a paper shop . . .

He laid the glass on the desk, picked up a squash ball and squeezed it. The trick was to keep the fingers working. The squash ball was a tension breaker. He needed it, like he needed a cigarette smouldering in the ashtray and a bourbon by the Olivetti.

He sighed and walked to the window, stared into the dusk. Just write, Sloane had told him. Write something. Don't worry about winning Pulitzer prizes, just get something on paper.

Okay. He went back to the desk and reached for the bourbon glass. It had gone. He frowned. Could have sworn he'd left it by the typewriter. Maybe he'd taken it with him and left it on the windowsill. He turned to look and saw it on the bookshelf. Odd. He hadn't been over there. But he must have been. It couldn't have walked.

Must be the week of solitary confinement going to his head, some sort of sensory deprivation at work. He went to the bookcase, brought back his glass, and began to hit the keys: just write anything: *It was four in the morning. The phone rang, wakening the woman from a dreamless sleep*

He reached for the squash ball. It wasn't on the desk. He could have sworn . . . It must have rolled somewhere. Bourbon glasses can't walk, not unless they'd changed the laws of physics, but squash balls sure can roll. He scratched his head and bent below the desk, couldn't see it anywhere, then sat up to change the line he'd written. He didn't like 'dreamless sleep'. It was too author-ish. How would anyone but the woman know if she'd dreamt or not?

There was no paper in the machine. He blinked and shook his head. No sign of it. Then he saw it, on top of the pile of fresh paper. He picked up the top sheet.

It was four in the morning . . .

Jesus, he said. He had no recollection of tearing out the page. He stood up fast, knocking the chair back careening on its rollers across the floor, then he spun round. Susan must have come back and was playing tricks, or that little minx Lisa.

Now he needed the remains of the bourbon. He groped for it. Gone. He turned, bug-eyed, feeling an unaccustomed shiver run up his spine. It was on the windowsill. But he couldn't have put it there. No matter how many other minor memory blocks he had, he couldn't have gone over to the window since the last time . . . unless he had left it there before and simply imagined bringing it back with him . . . but no. None of this made sense.

He closed his eyes, leant against the desk and massaged his temples, told himself to get a grip on himself. It must be the booze. He would give it up from now on, start tomorrow sober. He'd have a bite to eat and an early night, start sober in the morning with everything nailed to the desk . . .

That decided, he got to his feet and made for the door, then stopped as he heard a hissing sound, something escaping, something under pressure.

'Goddammit,' he said aloud. 'Not a burst pipe now. Jesus Christ.' Grumbling to himself, he ran to the kitchen and looked in, then turned and stared up the stairs. The sound seemed to be coming from the landing. Still cursing, he ran up the stairs two at a time and stopped at the bathroom door. It was closed.

The sound was deafening now, the noise of a thousand angry snakes. He snatched at the doorknob, pulled and staggered back as a cloud of steam billowed into the hall, scalding his face and hands.

Baxter grunted in pain and bent at the knees, held his arm over his face and ran into the bathroom, holding his breath, feeling tears run down his hot cheeks. The steam was escaping from the hot water tap in the sink. He reached for it and yelped, drew his fingers back. The metal was red hot. Through blurred vision he reached for a towel, wrapped it round his hand and grabbed the tap again, spun it closed; but still the steam blasted out.

He dropped to his knees and looked under the sink at the S-bend. Drawing a lungful of hot, wet air, he spluttered and wheezed, grabbed the valve wheel and hauled at it, but it did not move. He could feel particles of rust coming away in his hands. Wrapping the towel round both hands, he strained at the wheel. Once, twice: nothing. Then he stopped, shivering in the heat. He was cold again, gooseflesh bubbling on his arms. He was caught in a grip of an irrational fear, an overwhelming feeling of claustrophobia, as if the walls were closing in on him, as if he were going to be crushed by the steam. He yelled an obscenity, yanked again with arms and shoulders, neck muscles straining, no longer caring whether he pulled the damned valve away from the pipe. It creaked and spun. Baxter grunted with relief, turned it twice and closed it. The steam was trapped. The noise ceased and he stumbled back on to the floor, sprawling on hands and knees, then turned quickly and rushed, stumbling, into the cool air of the hallway.

The air was like spring water. He gulped it, still shivering, then turned and looked back into the bathroom. There was no indication of any steam, no condensation. He touched his face, feeling for blisters, but his skin was cool. It was as if it had never happened. All that remained was the feeling of claustrophobia. Slowly he made his way down the stairs. His shirt was wet and stuck to his back and he was glad of it, otherwise he might have convinced himself that he was hallucinating. He pulled off his shirt and made for the bourbon again. Just one, he thought, then start sober in the morning.

NINE

Melanie's mind was in turmoil. She couldn't concentrate on anything and her work was suffering. On one occasion she had made the amateur's classic mistake of trying to take a shot without any film in the camera. She couldn't sleep and when she did, her subconscious turned traitor and woke her with grotesque nightmares. She was perpetually cold, even in well-heated rooms and outside in the sun. There were black smudges under her eyes, and she thought of going to see her doctor. But what could she tell him. That she had hallucinated in the Amityville house and now she couldn't stop shivering? He would say it was psychosomatic. It was all in the mind.

Then there was John. He was a stubborn man and she would not forgive him easily for failing to sympathize with her. His scepticism wouldn't let him understand and she would never be sure when he would look at her as if she had gone crazy. Perhaps she *was* going insane, and that was the scariest thing of all. Twice she had made the effort to phone him but the line was busy each time. Once she had got through and heard him pick up the receiver, but then the line went crazy with static and she had hung up; but she needed to see him. She had to make him understand that he was in danger as long as he stayed in that house.

That evening she finished work, declined the offer

of a drink from one of her colleagues and took a cab to the Village. She couldn't remember going into the bookshop. She must have wandered in absent-mindedly, but such things were common these days. She was forever finding herself in places, losing snatches of time, her day punctuated by gaps of memory.

What brought her joltingly back into the present was the sight of the house, a dozen of them staring at her from a display bin. It was the story of the Amityville murders, and behind the bin, on the shelves, a series of sequels. She reached out to pick up one of the books then turned away, fighting her curiosity, but it was too strong. She bought four books, rushed back to her apartment, prepared herself some cold meat and salad, opened a bottle of wine and began to read.

It was all there. It had all happened before and, as she read, she trembled uncontrollably. She read about the DeFeo murders and the theories that the young man had been possessed, the unanswered question, the riddle of how six people could be killed in their beds. Why had the others not been wakened by the first shot? Why had the neighbours heard nothing?

She read about the family that left in terror after only a month in the house. The story was too close for comfort. She reached into a drawer and began to make notes, underlining passages in the books. The static on the phone had happened before, stopping a priest getting through to the house. Doors and windows had closed by themselves. Others, before her, had hallucinated. Others had felt continually cold. She shivered even as she read this; and then the scariest thing of all: whatever evil there was in the house was not confined to the premises. It had followed people before, right across the country. There was no escaping it.

She read through the night and fell asleep in her chair as the dawn broke. Three hours later the phone rang.

She awoke startled, unsure where she was, grabbed the phone and grunted into the receiver. It was Elliot West telling her that nothing had shown in the tests.

She wasn't surprised.

'So, where do we go from here?' she asked.

'Nowhere. It's a dead end, I'm afraid.'

'Would you say this was one of your three per cents?'

'I honestly don't know. There's certainly no rational explanation.'

'So, what do we do?'

'File it,' he said.

'That's all?' She rubbed the sleep from her eyes, tried to think, tried to recall something she had read during the night. 'Can't you investigate the house?' she asked. 'You've got the equipment after all.'

'We could,' said West, 'but we'd need John's permission and I don't think he'd give it. Do you?'

'No. Not John Baxter.' She yawned, thanked him and asked him to send the prints and the camera to her office by cab. She'd pay. She just wanted to see them again, as soon as possible.

Two hours later she was leaning over an enlarger, pulling one of the prints out and pinning it to the wall. It was one of the shots of Sanders by the well, blown up as far as it would go, five feet by three, each grain the size of a dime. Close up, it was just a mass of greys and blacks. She stared at it for fully five minutes, at the mist that obscured Sanders's face, then unpinned it and took it to a glass table, spread it out and flicked a switch. The print was lit from beneath. Again she stared at it, frowning, trying to make sense of it, then picked up four strips of black masking tape and began to study it in sections, moving the black square around the print. It was like looking into a fire and seeing things in the flickering flames.

She moved the tape to the centre of the fault, where Sanders's mouth would have been if it had not been obscured. There seemed to be some kind of pattern in the frame, blurred lines and contours, grey lines running through the white mist. It took shape only when she stepped back a couple of feet, then she thrust her knuckles into her mouth to stop herself from screaming. The image was faint but discernible. It was a face emerging from Sanders's lips, a grotesque gargoyle of a face; black, sightless eyes, a leering toothless mouth, the same face she had seen in the house before the frost had taken a grip of her. She stumbled back against a developing tank, knocking it over, spilling a jar of fluid, coughing and spluttering at the smell of it, and now she knew what she had to do. She'd got her evidence and she knew where she had to take it. She had to confront the evil in its lair, and she had to get John Baxter out of that cursed place.

At first the car would not start. She swore and pumped the accelerator, damned and blasted, fidgeted in her seat, the print of Sanders in an envelope on the passenger seat.

The car started suddenly and shot forward a couple of feet. Again she cursed, forgetting she had left it in gear. The jolt sent the envelope on to the floor. She picked it up, laid it on the passenger seat and eased the car up and out of the office car park towards the slip road that led to the Queensborough Bridge. It was dark. She checked her watch; almost midnight. She had had to do a job before she could get out to Long Island. It would take her an hour to get to John, two minutes to get him out of there, and with luck they'd be back in the Village by two.

Maybe he wouldn't listen; but she dismissed the idea. It was unthinkable; she wouldn't even consider it. Her fingers danced on the wheel as she eased the car through the deserted streets. Manhattan still buzzed with traffic but in the outer boroughs, the people slept. She should have a clear road to Amityville. She hit the accelerator and took a turning too quickly, the car drifting. The steering wheel bucked in her hand as if alive and for a second she lost control, then drove into the skid, held it and glided round the corner.

'Take it easy woman,' she said aloud, reached for a cigarette and lit it with trembling fingers. A solitary drunk watched her and waved. 'Gotta be more careful,' she said, scolding herself, forcing herself to slow to fifty.

Her nerves were bad, ten times worse than the night she and John had gone to that phoney seance. If she'd known then what she knew now, she never would have gone near the place, never would have left the office. She pushed a button on the radio, looking for something gentle to soothe her nerves, but all she got was static on every channel, a road drill in her brain.

'Mighta known,' she said aloud, snapping the radio off. Now there was only the gentle purr of the engine, a mile of silence, then a different sound began to compete with the engine. Melanie frowned. There was a buzz in the car. Christ, she thought, don't tell me the engine is seizing up . . . but it was coming from inside. She checked the radio but it was off; then she saw it, a fat fly circling the inside of the car before settling on the windscreen.

She shuddered and slowed to thirty, keeping one eye on the fly, the other on the road. It was clear ahead but something was obscuring her view. She frowned, rubbed the windscreen with her sleeve, then jerked her hand back to the wheel. The windscreen was frosting over. She fought the panic that was beginning to grip her and turned on the fan heater, breathed a sigh of relief as it came on and began to melt the ice.

But how did the fly get in? The windows were closed. Maybe through an air vent or something. Maybe it had been there all the time. She looked back at it, just in time to see it zip into her face. She slapped at it, jerking the steering wheel, sending the car slewing across the road.

Bastard, she grunted as she straightened up. Again the fly came for her eyes and she swatted it away, keeping one hand firmly on the wheel. It's trying to kill me, she thought. The tiny black bastard is trying to kill me.

Then it was gone. There was no more sign of it. The buzzing had stopped. She thanked God and clutched the wheel, staring at the road ahead. Half a mile on she could see a construction site, blazing with light. On the ramp stood a trailer, loaded with steel girders. She held the car steady at forty, knuckles white on the wheel, then sniffed. Something was burning. She turned and saw smoke rising from the envelope. Now what? Her cigarette was safely lodged in the ashtray. She blew at the smoke, sending it drifting towards the door, looked back at the road for a second, then back again at the envelope. A tiny blue flame, like a candle flame from a child's birthday cake, had sprouted in the centre of the envelope.

Jesus, she said, and slapped at it. The flame grew bigger and brighter and she winced in pain as something burned her arm. She looked down and saw another flame appear on her sleeve. Without thinking, she took her hand off the wheel to slap it out, and the car went into a skid.

Now she was acting without thought, grabbing the wheel with both hands, trying to ignore the pain in her arm, choking in the smoke. The wheel jerked to the right and she couldn't hold it. She pumped the brake but there was no response, reached for the handbrake and pulled, jerked back as it came away in her hand. The envelope was now a mass of flames and the car was heading towards the trailer. She could see the girders protruding from it, and she tried to slither down her seat, but the seatbelt held her body rigid, so that all she could do was to bend into the windscreen, her arms round her head, two slim brown arms as protection against a ton and a half of steel coming towards her at thirty miles an hour.

The windscreen shattered and she was thrown forward, whiplashed back, her scream mingling with the screech of torn metal and the light tinkle of imploding glass. Then silence . . .

. . . the crash woke the young hobo who had been sleeping under sections of plasterboard by the gate of the site. He rubbed his eyes on a filthy sleeve and crawled to his feet, a mess of a man with matted, tangled hair and beard, ragged and barefoot. The sight in front of him made him blink; a red car concertinaed into the back of a trailer, the longest of the girders piercing it through the windscreen and out the back window, the red warning flag still fluttering at the end of the girder.

He thought of a skewer through a piece of meat and the image made him feel hungry. Slowly he trudged the ten yards towards it, scared of what he might see. He never could stand the sight of blood.

As he reached the car, he saw a woman struggling in the driving seat with a seatbelt. Smoke was rising through the shattered windscreen. He moved forward to pull her clear, then stopped in bewilderment. The woman was burning. Small blue flames sprouted from her hair, her body and her legs. She turned and looked at him, seemingly untouched by the crash. The girder had gone through the passenger side. It was a pretty face but made hideous by pain and terror. He tried to move towards her but his legs wouldn't function, and so he stood there as she pleaded silently with him, until the smoke filled the car and he could no longer see her; and still he stood, motionless, a helpless spectator watching the black smoke drift lazily through the windscreen and away, caught in the night breeze.

He did not know how long he stood there. It could have been ten seconds or sixty. He closed his eyes and lost track of time. When he opened them, the fire had gone out. He reached forward for the door handle. It was cold. He pulled and the door swung gently open.

'Jesus,' he whispered, as the smoke drifted past him. There was no sign of the fire. Nothing inside the car was burned, except the woman, strapped in to her seat, mummified by fire, a charcoal dummy, eyeless, black charred lips grinning in death.

He stepped back and retched, over and over, then looked up as a hand touched his shoulder. It was the night watchman, looking past him at the wreck, asking him what that hell had happened.

The hobo shook his head and lurched away. Briefly the watchman looked at him then stepped towards the car, just as the petrol tank exploded, hurling him on to his back, the flames singeing his face. On his knees he watched, horrified as the flames spread to the trailer, then he ducked as a second explosion lit up the sky. Night turned into day. He grabbed the hobo by the coat, his fingers slithering on vomit.

'Is anyone in there?'

The hobo couldn't answer.

'I said, is there anyone . . .?'

There was a third explosion as the flames reached the trailer's reserve tank and his words were lost in the blast. He turned away, realizing that his question did not matter now. If there was anyone in there, it was far too late to help.

A.3–D.—6

TEN

Baxter's head was throbbing. He had been on the phone all morning offering and receiving condolences. Now it was Nancy's turn. She had called to say how sorry she was but the words sounded forced. She was worried and it wasn't about Melanie. Melanie was past tense. To his surprise, Baxter found that he was defending himself.

'She'd been working late,' he said in a whisper. 'She wasn't coming to the house. She was nowhere near the house.'

'So, you see nothing strange?' she said, her voice flat and emotionless. 'The fact that two people . . .'

'Oh for God's sake,' he snapped. 'You sound just like . . .' He stopped himself in time and Nancy filled in the gap. '. . . like Melanie, you mean?'

He bowed his head and for a moment there was silence. He did not know if Nancy was blaming him, and at that moment, he did not care. He was perfectly capable of blaming himself.

Nancy broke the silence.

'John, I just want to say one thing and I know this is not the time, but I don't want there to be any misunderstanding between us. My daughter is the most precious thing in the world to me. She is not going into that house again. I've forbidden it.'

'She's my daughter too you know. You tend to forget that.'

'I'm not arguing with you.' He said, losing patience with her. 'I've told you the way it's going to be.'

'And I'm telling you that I've got some say in this.'

'Then say it to my lawyer.'

She hung up and he gazed at the receiver, thinking that maybe he would never speak to his wife again. A chapter had closed. Then he glanced at his watch. He had to hurry if he was going to hear the coroner's verdict.

Two hours later he came out of the courthouse, arm in arm with Elliot West, his mind in confusion.

'What I can't understand,' Baxter was saying, 'was that eyewitness sticking to his story. He was pretty convincing.'

'Didn't convince the coroner,' said West. 'I mean, he didn't exactly look convincing, did he?'

'Yet he insisted that only Melanie had been affected by the fire, that the car wasn't touched. Before the explosion, that is.'

'It's not a completely unknown phenomenon,' said West.

Baxter sighed. He'd heard of spontaneous combustion. He remembered seeing a book and grisly photographs of a woman in a fireplace. She had suddenly burst into flames. The theory was that victims had a stomach ulcer that generated methane gas. One heavy meal too many and you get combustion. But Melanie had never had an ulcer.

'I hate to admit it, but this whole thing is beginning to get to me,' Baxter confessed.

'In what way?'

'I just can't accept the idea that the damned house is responsible but . . . well, there's Melanie's pictures of Sanders. Even you say they're inexplicable.'

West nodded. 'There's no technical reason we can find. That's true.'

'Sanders dies in the house. Melanie insisted she had some sort of weird experience that night.' He stared across the road at a young, cheerful woman clutching a pile of parcels. She looked a bit like Melanie. 'I feel as guilty as hell.'

West watched him go. There was nothing he could do for the man except offer sympathy. Meanwhile he had to get back to the lab. and confront another Baxter. Nancy had called, asking to see him. He had been surprised to hear from her because they had never got on too well. She was friendly enough in a cold-blooded way but there was an aloofness about her that made friendship difficult. He could well understand why the marriage hadn't worked.

It was a short drive to the lab and he had just arrived when the intercom buzzed. Nancy Baxter was in reception. He stood up when she walked in. She oozed tension. Something was making her anxious. She was no longer the self-confident creature he had met in the past.

They shook hands and he noticed that her fingers trembled.

'Dr West, it's good of you to . . .'

The squawk of the intercom interrupted her. West smiled apologetically and pressed the switch.

'Sir, the s.d. in lab two is approaching crisis.'

'Okay,' he said, 'be right there.'

Nancy looked at him as he moved quickly from behind his desk, her face a question mark.

'Perhaps you'd like to see this,' he said, took her arm and guided her out of the room, along a corridor and through a door marked 'Control'. The room was dark. Nancy barely noticed the computer panel and the sound system. Her attention was focused solely on a wall of glass, through which she saw a woman lying on a cot, wearing dark goggles, and padded earphones. Electrodes were attached to her forehead, neck, chest and wrists. She was twitching, her mouth opening and closing like a fish.

West checked a chart and bent towards a microphone, but before he could speak, the woman sat upright, as if jerked by wires, and screamed.

'All right, that's it.' West's voice boomed through the mike into the laboratory. 'Get her out of there... and hurry!'

Two laboratory assistants in white coats ran to the cot, one stripping the electrodes from her, the other taking off the earphones and goggles, revealing a young woman, white faced, sobbing.

West turned to Nancy.

'She's been in there for fifty-two hours, about the limit for sensory deprivation. When you deprive the mind of all external stimulation, it begins to improvise.'

'So for more than two days, she's been in a kind of limbo?'

'Right. One of our students, a volunteer, by the way. She's been without sight or sound, nothing to touch, taste or smell. Under such conditions, reality has no objective meaning.' He smiled. 'Reality is a strange concept Mrs Baxter, the one word in the language that should always be used between quotation marks.'

She nodded trying to understand and he could see that she was interested. She kept staring at the woman on the cot.

Nancy Baxter was looking for answers. She wanted to believe that the mind could improvise, she wanted to believe in the power of hallucination. He began to feel like a priest in a confessional. Instinctively he knew that she was going to confess her fears to him, and once she had done that, she could no longer act the role of cocktail party hostess with the glass smile. The mask would be off.

'Shall we go back to the office?' he said.

She nodded and let him lead her back up the corridor, sat by his desk, declined the offer of coffee and came straight to the point.

'It's my husband's house,' she said. 'I have to know. Just the thought of my daughter going there terrifies me. I've read about it you know.' And she began to describe the stories about the house, ticking them off on her fingers. West held up his hand to stop her. He was well acquainted with them. There was no point in going over old ground.

'Look Mrs Baxter, all I can tell you is that there's no evidence that anyone has ever been directly harmed by the kinds of manifestations you are describing.'

'Meaning what?'

'Meaning that when there's been an injury or . . .' he searched for the word . . . 'a problem, it's always been from secondary causes, falling downstairs or running in panic.'

It wasn't what she wanted to hear. 'That's not exactly reassuring,' she said coldly.

'No. It isn't.' He paused, knowing that he was helpless, that there was not much he could do to calm her fears. 'I just don't have the answers you want. When we talk about spirits or ghosts, what do we mean? They may well be things people carry around with them, not things that hide in houses. On the other hand, certain places do seem to have an affinity for what we might call activity.'

'The Amityville house?'

'Possibly.'

'Has it ever been investigated?' she asked. 'I mean by reputable people?'

'Oh yes,' he said. 'Nothing concrete was found.' He hoped she wouldn't continue this line of questioning. He didn't want to have to tell her that a medium and a psychic researcher had become violently ill during a seance, in 112 Ocean Avenue, that a clairvoyant had claimed that she was aware of something negative in the house, something that had nothing to do with anything that was once human. It was something from the bowels of the earth, something that rested beneath the house, but had the ability to move beyond it. It would do her no good at all to know these things.

She shook her head and for a moment he thought she was going to cry.

'So many horrible things have happened,' she said. 'There must be a reason.'

'Perhaps there is. We simply do not know.'

She looked up at him, pleading. 'What do I do?'

It wasn't a question he could answer. He couldn't tell her to keep her daughter away from her husband. It wasn't something he could say. It was up to her and she knew it.

She thanked him and left. As he took her to the lift, they passed the young woman from the laboratory.

She looked exhausted, still white-faced, as if she had seen a ghost.

'Think about it, Mrs Baxter,' said West, watching her stare at the young woman. 'The imagination is incredibly powerful. Hallucinations can seem dreadfully real.'

She nodded and smiled at him as the lift door closed. He turned and went back to his office, thinking that he hadn't been much help to her. But he had done all he could. Her next appointment, he thought, would be with a psychiatrist.

ELEVEN

It was Lisa's idea to hold the seance. She had brought it up as they sat in a booth at Joey's Place, sipping cokes. Jeff and Roger had been talking dirty for twenty minutes, Jeff the big blond one, Roger small and dark, and she was getting bored. It looked as though Susan was going to get up and leave, and so she changed the subject. Why not a seance at the haunted house?

Susan shook her head. 'It isn't haunted.'

'Okay,' said Lisa petulantly. 'If you're scared.'

Susan hoped they would change the subject again. Even Jeff's stupid schoolyard sex jokes were better than this, but the boys wouldn't let it go.

Roger squeezed her arm. 'It's a fantastic idea,' he said. 'And you told us that your dad isn't home this afternoon.'

Trouble was, she liked Roger. He had tried to kiss her once and she hadn't let him, but she hoped that he would try again soon.

'Let's do it,' said Jeff. 'There's a bus in five minutes.'

'No,' said Susan. 'No way. Absolutely not.'

Less then an hour later they were standing in the hallway. Susan was scared and it was for that reason she had decided to do it, because it was childish to be scared, even by such an adolescent piece of nonsense like a seance. So she'd go along with it, not to show them, but to show herself.

Lisa had taken some of her father's typing paper and

was running upstairs, telling Jeff to look for a beer glass. No, no, she thought, not my room. She had already moved some of her stuff into the playroom in the attic and she wasn't going to let them go in there, not to her bedroom. That room was private. She caught Lisa at the second landing and grabbed her arm, pulled her away from the playroom door. Lisa shrugged. 'Okay, have it your way,' she said and pushed open the opposite door. The room was still bare, just four walls, rough floorboards and a window, the gauze curtain fluttering in the breeze.

As always Susan felt cold but she ignored it, reluctantly helped Lisa to cut letters out of the pieces of paper, each letter of the alphabet, Lisa instructed, plus 'yes' and 'no'.

That done, she scattered the letters on the floor, a confetti alphabet, smiled at the boys as they came in, Jeff clutching a glass beer tankard.

It was Lisa who took charge, telling people where to sit. Susan sat opposite, cross-legged with Jeff on the right and Roger on her left. The beer glass was placed upside down in the centre. 'Okay,' said Lisa when they had settled themselves. 'This only works if everyone co-operates and believes.' She looked at each of them in turn, told them to put one finger on the glass.

Three fingers touched the glass. Susan hesitated then did as she was asked. The glass felt cold. It was like touching an ice cube. Her finger seemed to stick to it; glued, frozen.

'We have to agree on a question,' Lisa was saying, 'and then concentrate very hard. The spirits will answer us.'

Her voice was deep, the same sepulchral tone she

had used before. The boys were fighting to suppress giggles.

'I'm going to ask the first one.'

Lisa closed her eyes and took a deep breath. 'Is there a supernatural presence in this room?'

Susan wanted out. Away from all this. It wasn't funny. There was nothing clever about it. It was stupid. So, she asked herself, if it's so dumb, what are you so scared of?

Silence. Everything was still for a moment; then the glass began to move. Jeff yelped and Lisa shushed him. The glass had moved some three inches towards a piece of paper with the word 'yes' scrawled on it.

'How about that?' whispered Roger.

'You're pushing it,' Susan shouted. 'Somebody's pushing it.'

'Nobody's pushing it,' said Lisa. 'It's moving by itself. Can't you feel it?'

They stared in silence for a moment at the glass, then Jeff grinned. 'I've got a good question,' he said, winking at Roger. 'Can it tell us the colour of Lisa's panties?'

'Forget it, Jeff,' said Roger. 'Everyone knows that.'

The tension evaporated in laughter. Lisa stuck out her tongue.

'Okay,' she said. 'A different question. Is there anyone here still a virgin?'

Susan groaned. It was all too silly for words. At times like this, she wondered if she were not far too mature for her friends. Their jokes didn't make her laugh, and Lisa looked so silly, posing on the floor like some smartass hooker or something. It was all too childish. She decided that she would just have to wait for them to grow up.

'Okay, okay,' said Jeff mischievously. 'Calm down. I've got a serious one.' They waited in silence. 'Is anyone round this table going to be dead before next year?'

Susan jerked back, pulled her finger from the glass.

'Don't ask things like that!' she said, her voice shrill.

Roger grinned at her. 'Hey, you're really scared, aren't you?' He tried to pounce on her but she slapped him away, stood up and moved to the door. Jeff looked up at her, pleading, asking her not to spoil things. She shook her head and backed away, then Lisa held up one hand.

'No, Susan's right,' she said. An unexpected ally. She reached for her and pulled her back to the circle. 'No more dumb questions. It's you guys who are wrecking things. All we do is ask the spirit who it is and what it wants.'

Again Susan gave in, sat cross-legged again, trying not to tremble. Again they touched the glass and Lisa claimed the floor.

'Is there anyone here in danger?'

Susan yelled at her, annoyed at being tricked. 'That's not what you said you would . . .'

She stopped in mid-sentence. The glass was moving towards an S, then a U and back to the S.

'One of you is pushing it,' she whispered. As if in response, three fingers were drawn back from the glass. Susan tried to drag hers away but it was stuck again, frozen to the glass. She felt the cold running up her arm into her shoulder and shivered. Her teeth clattered together. She had never felt so cold. It was as if ice was creeping through her body.

She gazed at the glass. It had stopped moving. She looked at the others, a silent plea for help, but they just stared back at her and she was reminded of doctors and a nurse staring down at a patient; then a second image came to her mind; they were mourners around a grave; they had that unique expression of grief, each one looking at her, desolate, mournful, as if she were dead.

She opened her mouth to say something, to ask them to pull her away, then felt the glass tremble. She glanced back at it, just in time to see it slip out from under her finger and fly across the room, two feet in the air, as if someone had hurled it, then smash into the wall, shattering into countless splinters.

'I didn't do it,' she said.

They did not answer, just stared from her face to the glass.

'Let's get out of here,' she said, and they nodded as one, waited for her to leave the room, then followed, some six feet behind her, as if they didn't want to get too close, as if she were contaminated.

It was only when they were out by the pool that they spoke. It was a relief to be out in the sun. Jeff and Roger began wrestling playfully, and Lisa put an arm round Susan.

'I'm cold,' Susan said.

Lisa smiled at her, not knowing what to say.

'We won't do that again,' she said at last.

'Oh no. Of course not.' It was a statement of fact.

The boys ran to the boathouse and the girls slowly followed them. Susan turned and gazed back at the house then up at the sun. It didn't warm her. It was as if someone had pulled the plug on it. None of the others seemed to be cold. The boys were running around in their T-shirts as if it were the height of summer. Then she remembered. It *was* the height of summer.

By the time the girls reached the boathouse, Jeff was whooping with delight. He had found a small green boat moored to the short jetty. It was a fragile looking thing with an outboard motor. Susan hung back as the others climbed in and began rocking it, making waves. It didn't look safe. Jeff pulled at the starting rope and the engine turned on the third attempt. He looked up and held out his hand to her. She didn't want to get in. All she wanted was to be somewhere warm with her father; but they were insistent. What was wrong with a trip on the river, they asked? There were other boats out there. It would be fun.

She managed a smile, took Jeff's hand and sat next to Lisa.

'This is more like it,' said Roger as the boat chugged into the current. Susan looked back into the wake and saw ice forming behind them, following them deeper into the current, a thin trail of ice stretching back to the jetty.

'I'm cold,' she said, but her voice was carried away by the wind, and no one heard her.

All afternoon Nancy Baxter had been unusually anxious. Much of the time she managed to push the anxiety away but today was different. It was a mental toothache that would not go away. It was Susan. Nancy wished that she was in the house or somewhere close where she could be seen but she had been out of the house for a couple of hours and Nancy knew that something was wrong.

She went to her daughter's bedroom and sat on her bed, looking at the photos of her as a little girl. There was a large print of John by the bed and she gazed at it sadly, thinking of unfulfilled hopes and wasted years. She picked up one of Susan's old dolls. It felt cold and as she stared into the glass eyes, the feeling that something was wrong intensified. She got up and looked out into the garden, leant out and called Susan's name. There was no reply.

Maybe she was with Lisa. She had a flash of the woman in West's laboratory and she scolded herself, told herself to act her age, but it was no good. She had to find Susan. If there was such a thing as telepathy, then it was working at full power. Susan was in trouble and calling for help. She was as sure of that as she was of anything; and in an instant she knew that her daughter had disobeyed her.

Suddenly the phone rang. It was Lisa's mother, wondering if Nancy knew where Lisa was.

'I think I know where she might be,' Nancy managed to say. Then she hung up and ran out to the car, praying that her intuition, or whatever it was, was sending out false signals. But deep down she knew it was not.

It took her half an hour to drive to Amityville. She was a careful driver but at one intersection she pulled out too quickly and almost hit a truck. She lit a cigarette but it slipped from her fingers and she had to tread on it fast before it burned a hole in the carpet.

The radio was playing Country and Western, but as Nancy turned into Ocean Avenue, it buzzed irritating static at her and she turned it off. She checked the numbers on the mail boxes and turned into the driveway of 112. It was the first time she had seen it and she looked up at it without curiosity. All she wanted was to get her daughter out of there.

The trouble was that she did not know what she was going to say to Susan. She didn't want to cause a scene and make her daughter look foolish in front of her friends. She would just have to play it by ear. Whatever happened though, she wasn't leaving without her.

She shut off the engine and basked for a moment in silence, then slowly got out and tried the front door, swallowing her fear of the place. It was daylight after all and no one came to harm during the day. The night was the time for horror, surely. It was tradition.

The door was locked. She moved to a window but could see nothing through the gauze curtain. Try the back. She went around the house glancing across at the river. She could see boats, and hear laughter mixed with the shrieking of gulls.

The back door was unlocked and she stepped inside, calling her daughter's name, moving cautiously, wondering what she would say if John were at home. What if he were not alone? She looked around the kitchen, picking up the new utensils he had bought and wondered if another woman had been there, cooking, washing up. The intimacy of the place disturbed her. She and John had become strangers but the sight of this comfortable little nest he had built himself made her sad. She couldn't help but recall the early days of their marriage when they were building a nest together . . . suddenly she stopped in her tracks, conscious of a chill, as if she had caught an instant fever. She spun round.

'Susan? Are you here? Susan?'

She hugged herself and without warning or apparent reason began to cry, 'Oh Susan, where are you?'

Repeating her name over and over, as if saying the word would banish her fear.

The sight of Nancy's car in his drive caused Baxter to grunt in annoyance. Why had she turned up uninvited? Was she snooping, trying to catch him out in some way? He slammed the car door and ran to the house, then stopped as he heard shouts from the river bank. He turned and shaded his eyes, saw three boats bobbing side by side. Two men were leaning over the side of one of the boats, pulling at something in the water, pulling out what looked horribly like a body. He could see his boat, the little green skiff with the outboard. Seagulls shrieked at him as he began to run.

It took the boats a couple of minutes to reach the jetty where Baxter was standing, his mind coming up with questions he couldn't answer. It was not until the green boat was close that he recognized Lisa. He hadn't been looking for Lisa and the sight of her surprised him. She was looking down into one of the other boats and he thought he could detect panic in her face.

Oh God. No God. Please God.

He ran to the end of the jetty and caught a rope thrown to him by a man he had never seen before. As he ran it through a brass ring, he caught sight of something in one of the boats, something bloated wearing a T-shirt and jeans. He hauled the boat to the jetty and stood back as the stranger jumped ashore. Another man was moving the body, lifting it towards him. He grabbed it and looked into Susan's puffy face. The eyes were open, staring sightlessly at him. It was the fact that they were open that frightened him. Why, if she were just asleep, were her eyes open? If she was asleep, then why, God, why? As he laid her on the jetty he realized he was shouting, coaxing her to wake up.

The stranger helped him lay her on her back and Baxter crooned into her face, telling her that it would be all right now. He was with her. Susan's hand was cold. He looked up. Lisa and two boys he recognized had clambered on to the jetty and stood motionless; scared little children. There were three others, two men and a woman.

'Call an ambulance,' he yelled.

'It's being done,' said one of the men.

From somewhere a blanket was produced and Baxter laid it over his daughter.

'Come on honey, you're all right now. It's Dad. I'm with you.'

He felt a hand on his shoulder and looked up to see one of the men bending over him.

'Let me try,' he said.

At first Baxter didn't understand, then he grasped the man's meaning. Together they turned Susan on to her stomach and moved her head to one side, then Baxter stood back and watched as the man pressed hard on Susan's back and lifted her elbows. Green water tricked from her mouth and Baxter prayed, for the first time in his adult life, praying for the skill of the stranger and the life of his daughter.

Nancy had made a tour of the house and stood now beside Baxter's desk. She touched the framed photo of Susan and looked at another of John and herself when they were younger. It was a piece of history, as if he wanted to remember only the good times. She wondered where he had put the recent photos. They were probably lost in a drawer. It was understandable. The smiles on them were forced.

'It was four in the morning . . .' she read aloud. At least he had made a start. That was something. She flipped through the pile of paper, seeing scribbled notes, hieroglyphics in shorthand, meaningless to her.

The front door opened and she turned, looked over her shoulder.

'Susan?' The smile fluttered anxiously. Was it Susan?

She dropped the papers and ran to the door, looked out into the hall and saw her daughter walk past her. She was soaking, dripping water, leaving puddles behind her as she crossed the hall towards the stairs.

'What on earth?' said Nancy, trying to stop her but she had reached the stairs now and was beginning to climb.

'Why are you all wet? What happened?'

Susan turned and smiled at her but said nothing. Her hair was sodden on her scalp and hung like rope on her shoulders. Traces of weed clung to her T-shirt. For a moment she stood looking at her mother then turned again and made her way to the first landing.

'Susan, I'm talking to you . . .'

No response.

'Susan. Answer me.' Nancy shouted in frustration. What was wrong with the girl? She followed her up the stairs and saw her moving up towards the attic.

'Susan!' Louder this time, the tone of command. Now Nancy was frantic. She had never seen her daughter act like this. Maybe she was in a state of shock. She stumbled panting after her and by the time she had reached the attic bedroom, the door had been

A.3-D.—7

slammed shut. She reached for the handle. It was locked.

Again she spoke her daughter's name. Again there was no reply. This was ridiculous. She knew all about adolescent moods and tantrums. She'd had her share of them herself. But Susan wasn't like that.

She glared at the door as if hoping that the force of her anger would permit her to see through it.

'I'm not leaving this place until you come out. Do you hear me?'

She turned and went back downstairs, almost slipping once on the puddles. Muttering angrily to herself, she decided to make a cup of coffee then try again. She would sit it out. Before long the wretched girl would have to come out.

Reaching the entrance hall she stopped, hearing the wail of a siren. Just like the old days in Manhattan, she told herself. She went to the door and looked out. The ambulance was close; too close for comfort. It sped past the house, throwing up gravel and made for the river bank. She followed it and saw the crowd on the jetty, then began to run. Boating accidents were horrible. She'd once seen a boy badly hurt when his kayak was run down by a power boat and she hoped she'd see nothing like it again.

As she drew closer, she began to recognize faces; a couple of boys Susan knew; and Lisa; but why was she crying? She pushed between two men and saw her husband kneeling beside something covered by a blanket. Two ambulancemen were pulling a stretcher from the back of the ambulance but hesitated when they saw Nancy. She frowned, wondering what John was doing down on his knees. She went up to him and tapped his shoulder, asked him what was going on.

He looked up at her and she took a step back. He was crying and she had never seen him in tears. He got to his feet and hugged her and the words in her ear were garbled.

'Nancy. It's Susan.'

She stepped back from him again, pushed him off. 'What about Susan?' she said sharply.

He glanced towards the blanket and stepped in front of it, shielding it from her with his body. The sobs shuddered through him and when she touched him, he was cold and wet.

'What are you saying,' she asked, irritated. 'You're saying that that . . .' she pointed to the blanket, 'is Susan?'

She shook her head.

'Susan's in the house, John,' she said and held his hand, trying to soothe him. 'I just left her in the attic.'

Baxter looked at her blankly, then back at the blanket. He could not speak. He held on to her and she struggled but she could not get away from him, and now she was yelling at him, telling him to let her go. She looked for help at the others but they just stood and stared at her as if she were crazy.

Lisa was shaking her head, tears running unchecked down her face while the boys stood motionless, in shock. The ambulancemen laid the stretcher next to the blanket and looked up at her.

'You can't tell me that that's Susan,' she said to the crowd, looking from one face to the other. 'I saw her. I was with her. She's in the house, soaking wet. She's changing . . .'

Her voice rose as she spoke until she was yelling at

them. Why did they not believe her? What was wrong with them all?

'All right,' she said at last. 'See for yourselves then.' She turned and pulled Baxter behind her, marched back towards the house, shouting at them to follow. Baxter did not resist. He stumbled behind her like a child being led by its mother while she muttered angrily that it was all nonsense. He would see when he got to the house.

The front door was still open and she ran inside, leaving Baxter slumped against the door. By the time she got to the attic, she was breathless. The door to Susan's room was open. She stepped inside, smiling, trying to catch her breath.

The room was empty. She clenched her fists and shook her head angrily.

'Why are you hiding from me, Susan?' she muttered, going to the closet and opening the doors, looking for her wet clothes.

She looked under the bed and ran to the other room, then down the first set of stairs to the landing, checked each room, her anger building into panic.

'I know you're here,' she shouted. 'Where are you?' She kept up a running monologue as she went from room to room, banging doors, skipped down the stairs, two at a time to the hall, making a mental note that the puddles had dried which was lucky for John; it would save him mopping up. She checked the kitchen, dining room and bathroom. All empty, which meant, by process of elimination, that she must be in the living room. But there was only her husband, slumped at his desk.

Nancy stared at him, her hands clenching and unclenching, her body rigid with frustration.

'Why on earth is she hiding?' she said. 'Why?'

Baxter slowly got to his feet and crossed the room, tried to embrace her, but she pushed him away.

She turned again towards the hall. 'She's here somewhere,' she said. 'I should be with her. Why won't she let me be with her?'

Baxter followed her but she ducked away from him.

'Nancy. Please stop for a minute and listen . . .'

'No,' she yelled. 'Leave me alone. You don't even care where she is. I'm going up to her room.' She stopped in the doorway and turned, nodded at him, wagged her finger in his direction. 'I'll wait for her in her room. That's what I'll do.'

Then she was gone and Baxter slumped once more into his chair, the room out of focus through the blurred vision of his tears.

The sedatives that the ambulancemen had given him worked fitfully. He slept for an hour and woke groggily, stumbled out of the house towards the river. The wet patch where she had lain had dried, leaving only a shred of weed to mark the spot. He looked at the jetty blankly, his lips moving in soundless prayer. He was angry with himself. He should have dried her face properly before they took her away. It wasn't dignified for her to be seen with a wet face and pieces of weed on her T-shirt. She should have gone with more dignity.

He began to weep again and he did not fight the tears. It would be better for Nancy if she could weep. He hoped that when she came out of shock, she would be able to weep. It was natural, after all.

Time lost all meaning. He could not remember coming

back to the house, couldn't remember it growing dark. One moment there was bright sunlight, the next it was black as night. He was sitting by the desk, feet up looking through the window. There was a crescent moon and a few stars. Slowly, moving like an old man, he went to the kitchen, filled a glass with water and picked up the box of sedatives, then went up to the attic, the boards creaking under his weight.

Susan's door was closed. He gently pushed it open and tiptoed to the bed. Nancy's face was lit by moonlight. She was lying fully clad on the bed, clutching a doll. Her eyes were open and she stared at the ceiling. He sat beside her and stroked her brow but she did not react.

She was cold. He whispered her name, feeling closer to her than he had for years, affectionate and protective. He took two pills from the box and offered them to her, said they would help her to sleep.

She looked at him as if aware for the first time that he was in the room.

'I don't need them, John.' Her voice was calm. The storm had abated. Briefly she gazed at him, then turned her back on him and lay, facing the wall. He placed the pills and the glass of water on the bedside table.

'If you need anything,' he whispered. 'I'll be downstairs.'

As he left the room, he realized that what he needed was a stiff drink. The ambulancemen had told him not to mix booze with the pills, but he didn't care. He wasn't interested in what happened to him any more.

The first slug of bourbon choked him. He spluttered and stretched out on the couch in the living room. Lisa's garbled account of what had happened came back to him; how Susan just sort of rose from the back of the boat as if something was pulling her overboard, how she disappeared immediately, which meant, he thought, that she hadn't suffered. It had been instantaneous and that was some consolation. Lisa had stammered through her tears that she always thought people were supposed to go down three times but it was all lies, all bullshit.

She had spat the word out. It seemed incongruous coming from the mouth of a child. Bullshit, bullshit, she had yelled until one of the young men calmed her down; then she told him how the other boats had arrived, how one of the men pulled Susan out and scraped the ice from her face.

Ice! He dropped a couple of cubes into his glass and filled it to the brim. Why ice at this time of year? He gulped the booze and sniffed. Couldn't have been ice. Must have been weeds or something. Then he began to cry again. He cried for maybe half an hour, half the bourbon bottle. He wasn't conscious of topping it up. He just did it automatically, killing the pain, with the anaesthetic of alchohol. The house was silent . . .

. . . . he awoke startled, eyes snapping open and checked his watch. Three fifteen. The moon had vanished behind thick cloud and the house was no longer silent. He cocked his head and heard a strange sound, the gurgling bubbling noise of water under pressure, coming from the basement. He stumbled off the couch and fell heavily. One of his legs had gone to sleep. He massaged his calf, trying to get the blood flowing. It took forever, and the noise of the water was steadily increasing. He hoped it wouldn't wake Nancy and scare her. In her condition, it would tip the balance. He got up and limped to the basement door, no longer caring what he would see. The house could explode as far as he cared. Nothing mattered any more, now that Susan had gone; and to think that only a few hours ago, he thought that his book was all-important. The hell it was. It was just ego masquerading as self-respect, and anyway, who cared about the morbid philosophizing of some unknown hack?

He pushed the door open and blinked in the updraught of bright white light, far too bright for the single bulb that hung in the middle of the room. It was more like the force of a bank of high-voltage spotlights. Shielding his face with his arm, he slowly edged down the stairs. Half-way down he stopped, and gazed fascinated at the sight below. The well was open, the planks stacked neatly in a corner of the room. Above the well hung a ball of brilliant transparent light. Beyond it, shimmering as if in a heat haze, he could see the back wall and the steps leading to the storm door. For a few seconds he was blinded and did not notice the figure sitting by the well, not until it turned and looked up at him.

'Nancy!'

He gaped at her. She looked the same as she had done in Susan's room, except that now she was smiling. A word came to mind, a word normally associated with brides; radiant. Nancy looked radiant in the spotlight. She was beckoning him towards her with one hand and pointing down into the well with the other. He shook his head. He had no desire to go any further. All he wanted was to take her away, out of the house, but she was insisting, smiling sweetly at him, saying something, her voice no competition for the roar of the water.

Slowly, reluctantly, he made his way down the stairs. Nancy held her hand out to him and he clasped her fingers. They were cold, as if there was no blood in her. Her eyes sparkled and he lip-read one word: 'Look'. She was pointing again into the well.

He went down on his knees and peered into it. Water was lapping only a few inches from the top. The closer he bent towards it, the louder the roar and he was reminded of Niagara. Nancy, the radiant bride, holding his hand; the roar of Niagara and spray on his face. He wiped it off. It was ice-cold. He could feel ice forming on his eyelids and he rubbed them, feeling as cold as a corpse. When he opened them again, Nancy was pointing excitedly into the well, lips pouting, 'Look look, look', pushing him closer to the edge.

There was something in the water. Baxter narrowed his eyes, trying to make it out, a shape of some kind, deep in the wall, slowly rising to the surface in a lazy spiral. Panic began to build inside him like steam and he wanted to run, but his legs wouldn't obey. He tried to back away from the well but Nancy held his arm tightly; and now he could make out the shape. It was human. A girl. He could recognize the T-shirt and the jeans.

'Susan!'

The word lodged in his throat. He tried to close his eyes, shut out the sight of it, but they remained stubbornly open. He no longer had any control over his body. Nancy let him go and he found himself reaching down into the well, reaching for Susan, as the men must have done in the boat.

The body turned, face up, coming up fast now towards him, the face bloated and twisted, eyeless in the puffy cheeks. It was grinning at him, reaching out for him. He screamed and the thing screamed with him, a terrible discordant harmony as it propelled itself out of the water, grabbing for him with hands like claws, pulling him down into the water. For an instant he was aware of a putrescent smell, aware of the cold claws on his face, of Nancy pushing him from behind, then black ice-cold water choking him, and he knew he was going to die . . .

. . . he awoke slowly, drifting into the half light, coughing and spluttering, to see the bourbon bottle lying empty beside him. His hand was in the ice bucket. Slowly he lifted it, clutching a couple of ice cubes, placed them on his forehead and grimaced in pain.

The ambulancemen had been right. The booze and the sedatives had conjured up a nightmare. He swung himself off the couch and looked at his shoes. He hadn't even bothered to take them off. There was a line of damp around them, as if he had been walking in water. Yawning and stretching, he opened the curtains and stepped back, blinded by the dawn.

Coffee, he thought. Sweet and black. Before he reached the kitchen he could hear someone singing, a vaguely familiar tune; a lullaby.

He pushed open the kitchen door and stood motionless, shocked by the sight in front of him.

Nancy stood in the centre of the room, ironing a blouse, singing softly, looking like a housewife in a TV commercial. The similarity ended there. All around her was chaos. Drawers had been pulled open. Cutlery was scattered on the floor, glinting among the shrapnel of smashed crockery. Vegetables were strewn across the floor. The three chairs had been overturned. Sauce bottles had been sprayed on the walls as if some insane graffiti artist had been at work.

'What the hell?'

Nancy looked up at him, smiling, the same radiant smile of his nightmare. Radiant amidst the chaos.

'Susan,' she said. 'She wants to show us she's here.'

Baxter slumped against the door and Nancy held up the blouse she was ironing.

'It's her favourite. Remember, John? She got it two years ago for her birthday. It's the colour. I'd like to find her something this year, a cashmere sweater perhaps . . .'

'Nancy,' his voice was a hoarse grunt, fractured by the bourbon. 'You must try to grasp what's happened.'

'You mean what you say has happened.'

'You're fantasizing, Nancy . . . None of this is real any more. You're got to come to terms with that.'

Nancy looked at him calmly. 'For me, what I saw in this house, with my own eyes, is what's real. Fantasy it what you saw. Fantasy is Susan . . . drowned.'

She had gone mad, he thought. Quite mad. It was as simple and as tragic as that. He wanted to take her in his arms, but she was shooing him away and reaching for another blouse.

There was nothing he could say to her. Nothing that would help.

TWELVE

The coffin was borne by six of Susan's classmates, Jeff and Roger in the leading positions. The rain was light, hardly more than a mist, but enough to camouflage the tears running down the boys' cheeks. Baxter led the crowd of mourners to the graveside and stood in silence through the hymn and the preacher's ritual address. He had declined the offer of an umbrella, and the bible was damp in his hands. As the coffin was lowered, he looked to the sky, letting the rain wash over him, eyes closed, waiting impatiently for the ordeal to end.

Then it was over.

Neighbours from his married days filed past, punctuated by ex-colleagues from the magazine, each one whispering how sorry they were. He acknowledged each one until only Elliot West remained. The man had become a close friend over the past couple of weeks, almost constantly by his side the last two days. Previously he had been no more than an acquaintance, but since the death, first of Melanie, then of Susan, Baxter had come to rely upon him. He was the one common link, the man who seemed best able to understand his grief.

West took his arm and led him towards the limousine by the gate, waited while Baxter took one last look back at the freshly dug earth and the headstone with its simple statement:

Susan Baxter
1967–1983

It was such a short life, such a simple piece of arithmetic. He vowed there and then that he would visit the grave every day, so that she wouldn't be lonely.

They sat in silence as they were driven to Ocean Avenue and it was only as they neared the house that Baxter spoke.

'If only Nancy had come. She has to confront this. She has to face the fact, but she won't. She won't accept that Susan's lost to us.' He paused. 'I don't know what to do.'

It was a unique admission. Baxter had always been the epitome of self-reliance and self-control. He had never been known to admit to helplessness. Up until a few days ago, he had all the confidence in the world. Now he was a lost soul.

'There's always the possibility that she doesn't need help,' said West.

'Huh?' Baxter blinked. He wasn't expecting such a reaction.

'What if she really did see something? Not Susan maybe, but something.'

Baxter sighed. He looked at West blankly. What was going on? Was he the only sane one? Baxter shook his head. He knew that one definition of madness was the belief that everyone else was mad.

'After all that's happened,' he said. 'I don't know what the hell to believe.'

West considered Baxter for a moment and made a decision. Now was the time to put the idea to him, the idea that Melanie had come up with.

'Look John,' he said. 'If you'd go along with me, I'd like to try something. It could be helpful to you, to me and to Nancy.'

Baxter looked blankly at him, disinterested. 'What have you got in mind?'

'A scientific investigation of the house for psychic phenomena.'

Baxter continued to stare at him but did not react.

'I've got a trained team and all the latest equipment,' West continued, trying to enthuse the man, trying for a response. 'We've investigated places a lot less qualified than this house.'

'What would be the point?'

'Well, the chances are that we'd come up empty handed. If we do, it might make it easier for you to reason with Nancy.'

Baxter shrugged. 'Possibly, but not likely,' he said.

West felt his sympathy come under strain. Why was the man being so reluctant? What had he got to lose?

'Still,' he persisted, 'if we do turn up something . . . if there were some indication, no matter how ephemeral, that Nancy is right, then we might be saving her sanity.'

Baxter finally reacted. His eyes came to life and he glared at West. He had been torn for days between his natural scepticism and a basic unreasoning fear. He needed to lash out at something and West was the only target.

'This is all nonsense,' he roared. 'Nancy didn't see a damned thing.'

West glared back at him. 'How can you be so goddamned sure?' he said quietly.

For a moment the two men stared at one another, their faces only a few inches apart. It was a stand-off and it was Baxter who broke, slumping back into the couch, flapping one hand in front of his face. The resentment had flared and was gone and West's sympathy returned.

He knew now that Baxter was a defeated man and that he would agree to anything. The investigation would take place. The only question was when.

THIRTEEN

They came after dark in a convoy of trucks and cars. Baxter watched them from the attic, counted the headlights as they moved through the village and up Ocean Avenue. West hadn't wasted any time. No sooner had Baxter agreed to the investigation than he was on the phone making arrangements. He had insisted on doing it that very night. He didn't want Baxter to remain in the house any longer than necessary. If there was some 'activity', as he called it, he wanted it discovered before it did any more harm.

As he made his way downstairs, he wondered how many cancelled dates he had been responsible for that night, how many phone calls home saying that dinner would have to wait . . . and he thought back to West's little lecture before he went back to the Institute to organize his team.

He had talked about something called infestation, whereby psychic forces affected material things around the person under attack. He talked of psychokinesis, objects moving of their own accord. Baxter had heard the word. He had come across stories in his job. All of them had been faked. Had he noticed any manifestations in the house, West asked? Baxter remembered the bourbon glass and the piece of typing paper, but he didn't mention it to West. He had put it down to absent-mindedness.

Any hallucinations. No, he said.

Do you have a crucifix in the house?

No.

Any examples of infestation?

Such as? he had asked.

Recurrent swarms of flies?

No.

Windows and doors opening and closing on their own?

No.

Unnatural cold?

Baxter had nodded at that one and West had made notes, explaining the theory that psychic forces drew on body heat in order to boost their powers.

The final question made Baxter grimace. Had he noticed any excessive smell of human excrement?

Jesus Christ, Elliot, he had said. No way.

And then West had gone, saying he would be back that evening. Now he was keeping his promise.

Baxter opened the door and saw them park round the house and begin to unload their equipment, piercing the night sky with their chatter. He shivered and looked back up the stairs, heard the wind in the dead trees, heard the shutters creak as if the house were moaning, protesting in anticipation of the invasion.

West was the first to come in, shaking his hand and smiling encouragement.

'How are you? Anything new?'

It was his patronizing bedside manner and it irritated Baxter.

'No,' he said.

'Nancy?'

'No change.'

They stood back to let the first of the technicians come in. West began making introductions and Baxter nodded to each of them; a dozen young men and women, all very earnest. He soon lost track of the names.

'It will take some time to set up the equipment,' said West. 'Let's take a walk.'

They wandered in silence through the garden to the boathouse and back. The sky was black and heavy with clouds. The wind tugged at their clothes and Baxter was reminded of that first night. It was the same oppressive humidity, the night of the phoney seance. Now they were going to put the house to the test. He shivered and rubbed gooseflesh on his arms, felt a tremor of fear, thanked God for the feeling. He had thought that his emotions had dried up and atrophied. He had thought that he would never feel anything again. Even fear was better than being an emotional vegetable.

West, for his part, was thinking about Melanie and her last frantic phone call to him on the day she died, the grotesque description she had given, some vision of hell. She had made some crazy connection between this gargoyle and the story of the Indian chief, told him she had evidence and she would present it to him the next day.

He had pleaded with her to come and see him straight away but she had been determined to get to Baxter. He would never tell Baxter this story. It would do him no good to know that Melanie had gone over the edge and it would certainly add to his guilt if he knew she had been on her way to see him that night . . .

His thoughts were interrupted by one of his staff shouting from the house that they were ready for him. He felt himself tense up with excitement, then grabbed Baxter's arm and dragged him at a run to the house.

In the living room, Baxter shook his head and whistled in appreciation. In a matter of minutes, the place had been turned into something resembling Cape Canaveral. Five TV monitors had been set up above his desk. The coffee table was loaded with audio racks and ultra-sound units. Along the length of the far wall was a bank of computers and what looked to Baxter like a small telex machine. That, he thought, would be the print-out, the printed evidence of the data that would flit through the computers.

A video camera, an oscilloscope and an intercom were being connected up. Wires ran across the floor and out of the door and a thick cable led down into the basement.

West beamed at him. He was happy and excited, at home in his favourite environment.

Baxter turned and glanced up the stairs. A young sound engineer wearing headphones was sitting half-way up, checking the dials of a recording unit. Behind him, on the landing, a video cameraman was adjusting a lens. In the kitchen doorway a second sound man was tightening a nut on a directional mike.

Again West was at his elbow.

'What about the attic?' Baxter asked.

'It's covered,' said West. 'Every inch of the place is wired for sound, light and heat. Every sense is tapped. We're plugged into everything imaginable.'

He took Baxter's arm and led him to the control unit, tapped the mike and blew into it. His voice hissed through the house. 'Testing.'

Two male technicians and a young woman, all wearing identical white boiler suits, turned and looked at Baxter. The woman's name was Jenny. Hers was the only name he could remember. They all looked very earnest. West made his way to the intercom and tapped it.

'Is Jeff by the fusebox?' he asked the woman.

She nodded.

'Okay. Tell him to switch on.'

She moved to the basement door and shouted down. Instantly the TV monitors came alive, the microphone squealed and Baxter put his hands over his ears as feedback screamed through the amplifiers.

West turned to him. 'Okay, as well as TV, we've got ultra-sound sensors, a thermal camera that detects temperature variations, a spectrophoto fluorometer . . .'

'Huh?' said Baxter.

West grinned. 'In simple terms, it detects X-rays and measures colour intensity and wavelength.'

'Ah,' said Baxter.

West pointed to the computer bank. 'Everything is fed through here,' he said. 'If there's anything, any kind of manifestation at all, we'll pick it up. And through this,' he indicated the microphone, 'I can talk to everyone in the place.'

'Impressive,' said Baxter.

West leant into the microphone. 'Right,' he said. 'Cut video two. Let's see where we are with three.'

Baxter did not wait to see any more. He wanted to be with Nancy whether she needed him or not. As he climbed the stairs he greeted each of the technicians, watching them move to their allocated positions. The light was dull, each bulb covered by gauze. It was as if the house was out of focus, the shadows blurring into one another.

A video cameraman was standing on the attic landing and Baxter pushed past him to Susan's room.

Nancy was sitting stiffly in the chair beside the bed, eyes closed, clutching one of Susan's dolls. It was an old doll, the face scarred by countless falls. It was bald with a smiling rosebud mouth. One eye was missing.

Baxter crouched beside his wife and whispered her name. Her eyes opened and she gazed at him; an intense penetrating look as if she were trying to look into his soul.

'You've never believed in this house,' she said softly. 'Take care.'

Baxter could think of no response. He just watched over her as she closed her eyes again and turned to the wall. The doll squealed in her arms, a tiny cry, 'Mama . . .'

He pulled another chair to the bedside and stretched himself. Whatever happened, he would stay and look after her. It was his place. There was nowhere else for him to be.

Everyone was in position. Each piece of equipment had been tested. The eye of each camera was open, the senses of every technician straining to pick up a stimulus; a moment of calm, of suspended animation, of anticipation.

The only thing moving was a large black fly, soundlessly circling the living room. No one noticed it. It circled the room then moved out into the hall and up the stairs.

Barry Boyle, a young sound operator, was squatting by the banisters, trying to concentrate on the job, trying to forget the girl he had been forced to stand up that night. Something tickled his ear and he slapped at it, then shivered as he noticed a breeze wafting his hair. He reached for his radio.

'Location three. I've experienced a marked drop in temperature.'

Immediately West's voice responded, echoing through the house.

'Thermo and video one to location three.'

In the living room West felt himself tense up. The adrenalin was flowing. He could feel his heart-beat and the throb of a pulse in his temple. As he gazed at the computer bank, he was conscious of Jenny moving beside him, felt her breath on his neck.

One of the screens began to flash figures at him while the print-out started chattering, spewing out a tape, a printed record of the drop in temperature in location three.

Something was on the move.

West shifted his attention to the screen which showed a technician with a thermovision ray gun moving up the stairs, followed by a video cameraman. His pictures, in turn, were appearing on the adjacent screen. West's eyes flickered from one screen to the other, watching the men climb the stairs and pass Barry Boyle, saw the startled look on Boyle's face. He was clutching himself as if he had suddenly found himself in the heart of a blizzard.

'Don't wobble, video two,' he muttered. 'Keep the bastard steady.'

The whisper hissed through the house and briefly stopped the cameraman in his tracks. West watched him hitch the camera closer to his neck, then carry on climbing.

Now the thermo operator had reached the attic.

'Follow him, video two,' said West.

He stared fascinated at the screen, seeing Baxter stand up as the thermo operator came into the room, the camera catching his anxious expression, surprised at the intrusion, blinking at the sight of the ray gun pointing at him. Behind him, Nancy sat unmoving.

The voice of the thermo operator crackled through the amplifier.

'It's definitely registering.'

'We're reading you,' said West.

Jenny nudged him. 'The epicentre is sub-zero.'

'It's moving,' grunted the thermo operator, his voice trembling with excitement.

'Track it,' shouted West. 'Stand by video one.'

Silently he watched the man move back out on to the landing and down the staircase, the only sound in the room being the chatter of the print-out.

'Be alert everyone,' he said. He had never encountered such a force. He had a flash of memory. Only a few hours ago he had told Baxter about the meaning of sudden, apparently unaccountable sensation of cold, and had seen the look of scepticism on the man's face. Perhaps he would believe now. But where had it come from? Where was it drawing its strength from? From Nancy? Or Baxter? Or both?

He checked himself. This was no time for theorizing. He had to check the data. He could worry about the analysis later, when all the information was in. He yelled at his staff on the first floor landing to pick up the others as they came down, but they had anticipated him, the sound boom operator leaning towards them with a high powered directional mike, while a video cameraman caught the action.

He blinked, startled, as Jenny squealed something in his ear. She was pointing at one of the screens, at a glowing white light, above the frame line.

'Pan up Video two,' he yelled.

The operator obeyed. The light filled the screen and his voice boomed, an obscenity.

'What the hell is it?' grunted West.

It was the sound operator who answered. 'Some kind of light, hanging here on the stairs. Christ. Now it's moving down.' The screen was now so bright that they could hardly look at it. Jenny's face, reflected in the glare, showed the first signs of fear, the pupils dilated, mouth open.

'Can't focus,' said the cameraman. 'It's too bright.'

West swore beneath his breath, heard Jenny gasp. He turned. The light was in the doorway now, pulsing, blinding them. West shielded his eyes and turned back, keeping his gaze fixed firmly on the control unit, resisting the temptation to watch the light as it moved towards him. The dials were going crazy, flashing figures at him.

'Stay with it everyone,' he yelled, conscious of the tension in his voice, fighting to stay calm. If he were to break, then there would be chaos. It was a command, delivered with all the authority he could muster.

His crew did as they were told, two cameramen, the sound operator and the thermo operator tracking the light across the room, shielding their eyes from it, trying to keep their equipment steady.

And then it was gone, through the basement door.

'Video three,' he shouted.

'Got it.' The response from the basement was immediate.

'It's trapped,' West muttered to himself. 'We've trapped the bastard.' Then he shivered, feeling the cold for the first time.

He hadn't noticed it as the light passed. He was so full of adrenalin, but now that it had gone, he felt the chill. He shivered and looked up as Baxter came into the room. He was white-faced and walking stiffly, his lips moving. West frowned and moved across to him, grabbed his arm. Baxter's eyes were glazed as if he were sleep-walking.

'John,' said West sharply.

'The well,' he muttered. 'Susan's in the well.'

'Jesus,' West muttered, drew back his hand and slapped him hard across the face, hard enough to knock him back against the wall. Baxter shook his head and looked up, eyes focusing on him.

'What were you saying?' West asked. 'About the well?'

'I don't know.' His voice trembled. 'I had to follow the light, to get to Susan. That's all.'

'A dream,' said West.

'I don't know, Elliot.' He passed his hand over his brow. For a while he had lost all track of reality. He vaguely remembered leaving the room, drawn by some kind of magnetic force, but whether it was a dream, a hallucination or reality, he did not know. He had no longer any guidelines, and he felt tired, lethargy dragging at his eyeballs. He slumped to the floor and watched West go back to his control panel, saw him through blurred vision, his eyes smarting in the blazing light that shone from three of the TV screens.

'Got it,' West muttered. 'Three cameras on it.' There was a hint of triumph in his voice and, from the floors above, he was answered by a nervous spatter of applause.

Then the room darkened. The light went out.

'What the hell?' West's frustration echoed through the house.

'It's gone.' The voice of the cameraman in the basement replied. 'It's just disappeared.'

The dials had stopped moving. The print-out was silent.

Jenny looked up and shrugged. 'I'm getting nothing,' she said. If there had previously been a trace of triumph in West's voice, now there was relief in the words of his assistant.

West cursed and ran across the room to the basement steps, ran down, his progress picked up by one of the video cameramen, his voice floating up the stairs, answered by the amplified voices of his staff.

'Where is it?'

'It was here,' said the sound man, 'and then it wasn't.'

A pause, then, 'Go on back up. Go on.'

Baxter watched as the technicians appeared in single file at the basement door, trooping into the room, each one white-faced and shivering. He turned to Jenny.

'You lost it.'

She nodded.

He glanced at the monitor, saw West scurrying around in the basement.

'He shouldn't be alone there,' he said, but the woman was not listening. She was reading the print-out and shaking her head. What she read made no sense, unless you believed in the paranormal, and if you believed, as she did, then there was every reason to be terrified.

In her dream, Nancy was cold. The water was cold. She touched her face and scraped the frost from her eyes and mouth. She could see Susan clearly, outlined in a ball of white light. Nancy screamed because her daughter was hideous, the skin bloated and putrefying, and when she came towards her, the breath was foul. Susan was grinning, a toothless smile, the voice deep.

'Mother I'm here. You know I'm here. We'll be together now. We'll always be together.'

Nancy tried to move but her legs wouldn't obey. She tried to swim, but the current was dragging her down into the arms of the creature that once had been her daughter. She opened her mouth to scream and her mouth filled with water, foul, stagnant water, glutinous filth fouling her lungs and she knew she was going to die . . .

She awoke screaming, the doll staring one-eyed at her and smiling a rosebud grin. Nancy curled herself into a ball on the bed, knees drawn up, arms hugging herself. She gazed round the room and shivered, saw a fly on the window, watched as ferns of ice began to form round it, growing thicker, moving outwards across the glass. And now she was sure. Susan was dead. She would never see her daughter again. She began to cry and the tears froze on her cheeks . . .

Barry Boyle stumbled out of the living room into the hall. He had had enough. He did not know what the light was, and frankly he did not care. All he wanted was to get out. He'd had enough for the night.

He glanced up the stairs, bowing low against the wind that howled down from the landing. He had left his papers on the stairs, in a clipboard, and they were fluttering in the gale. He stopped and frowned in confusion. There seemed to be a film of frost on the banister, but that was impossible. He shook his head, trying to get rid of the image. It was absurd.

August 11th and frost inside a house. No. It couldn't be.

He turned and noticed a photograph of a young girl hanging in the hall. Must be the daughter, he thought, a bit plump, but pleasant enough; it was a tragedy that she had died so young. As he looked at it, the glass began to frost over. He turned and made for the door, then stopped again as he caught sight of himself in the hall mirror. It was a large sheet of glass, three feet square, and he looked strange in it. There was something wrong with his reflection; and then he realized. It too was beginning to freeze. He felt the frost nip at his nose and ears and stood motionless for a moment watching the glass film over with ice.

For an instant he found himself in a dilemma. He wanted to run but he knew he should stay and make his report; that was his job, after all.

'Hey Jenny,' he yelled. 'Ask Dr West to come . . .'

He got no further. The mirror shattered under the pressure of the ice, sending triangles of glass zipping through the hall. One piece caught him in the throat, severing his vocal chords, stifling his scream before it could build up. Another pierced his left eye. He staggered against the wall, clutching his face as blood pumped from his nose and mouth, instantly freezing and choking him. He slithered down the wall and briefly kicked out, a final spasm, a twitch of life, then he was still, while frost grew like ivy over his face.

The sound of shattering glass brought a cameraman running down the stairs. Barry Boyle had been a friend of his and he gasped as he saw the body, then he retched, the bile freezing on his chin. Slowly he backed away from the sight, towards the living room, scraping the obscene icicles from his face.

The others looked at him curiously as he came bursting into the room but he paid them no attention. He saw something they had not noticed. The TV screens behind them were frosting over. He yelled a warning and ran towards the screens, pushing Jenny aside in his haste. Reaching the nearest screen, he began scratching it with his thumbnail, trying to scrape the ice off, thinking that he would have to get the equipment out fast. It cost tens of thousands. He bent his knees, his arms round the set, ready to heave it on to his chest, so that his face was only an inch from the screen when it imploded, the force of the blast sending him tumbling against the coffee table, his head smashing against the steel base, concussing him. It was a merciful blow. Unconscious, he could not know that his face was filled with glass, nor could he feel the ice forming in the congealing blood . . .

Jenny could not move. She had been a nurse for a year and she knew that blood could not congeal so quickly. She turned and shouted down to the basement, yelled for her boss to come up and explain things. Dr West knew, would know what to do. He always knew what to do. He would explain that this was unreal, that it was just a nightmare. A movement caught her eye. The control panel was moving, caught in the wind that was howling through the door.

'Dr West!' It was no good. And then she remembered. He was still linked to the microphone. She could get him through the sound system. She bent towards it, just as the control panel broke from its sockets and smashed into her, cracking her skull and sending her sprawling into the back of amplifiers. Her last dying scream echoing, as feedback, a terrible screech, her eardrums bursting, perforated by the sound of her own voice . . .

Those who could move were yelling and running in confusion as computer parts were torn from their stanchions and zipped through the room like shells. Cables snapped in the air, snake-like in the gale, catching the technicians round their ankles, whipping at their faces as they fell. A young cameraman, lightly built and frail, was picked up by the force of the wind and hurled through the living room window, the glass lacerating his arteries, his blood spouting into the night air.

Throughout the chaos Baxter had acted instinctively, grabbing the heavy door as the gale broke around him, holding on to it with both hands, watching the carnage helplessly. Now he believed. He believed everything he had heard or read about this cursed place. His scepticism was in tatters, his mind a kaleidoscope of memories and guilt. It was he who had started all this. It was he who had agreed to this investigation, this sacrilege that had so enraged whatever evil inhabited the place.

He thought of Melanie and of Susan, and the memory of his daughter brought Nancy to the centre of his brain. He had to get to her. He spun round in the doorway and fell to his knees as the door was wrenched from its hinges and sent smashing against the opposite wall, then bounced off it, rearing like a paper kite into the ceiling, smashing again into the line of TV sets.

'Nancy,' he grunted. He would need to be single-minded now. A cable coiled round his leg and hauled him towards the centre of the room. He swore aloud, tore it off and crawled to the door. In the hall he moved over something grotesque, something that resembled a snowman, with glass in its eye and throat. He gagged, coughed and brought up bile, but did not stop. He had to get to Nancy.

He reached the stairs as the chandelier exploded like a giant firework showering him with glass shrapnel. He could feel blood on his cheek. Slowly he pulled the splinter out and dropped it, felt the blood cake around the wound.

Again he whispered his wife's name. He would get her out of this damned and cursed place if it was the last thing he did . . .

. . . In the basement, Elliot West was unaware of the chaos above, his headphones effectively deadening the noise. For a moment he had wondered why he was getting nothing through the cans, why the line had gone dead, then he had dismissed it. There were more important things to think of.

He probed each corner of the basement with the thermo unit, wondering if anything was registering upstairs. He doubted it. Whatever force there had been had simply vanished. But where? He squatted in the centre of the room, pushed back the headphones, and looked at the ceiling as he heard the commotion upstairs.

He turned and looked at the staircase. 'Now what?' he grunted to himself, what was he missing? He took one step towards the stairs, and got no further; something behind him was on the move. He was aware of a splintering sound. He turned and saw the planks above the well begin to move under strain. Nails pinged out of the joist and flew into the ceiling.

His first reaction was professional annoyance. Something was trying to force its way out of the well and there was no one around to help him record it. Why had he sent everyone away? It was sheer bloody carelessness. In that half-second, Elliot West felt no fear, then the planks were forced apart, spinning, cracking and the well was revealed, a gaping hole, a wound in the earth. Beams of light, brighter than any light he had seen, began to coil out of it, curling around his body and dragging him towards the lip of the well.

He screamed. There was nothing to fight against, nothing to grab hold of, and even as he screamed, a part of his brain was trying to rationalize and make sense of it, to determine what the energy was, for it would be a terrible thing to die and not know what your killer was.

The light blinded him, the roar from the well deafened him. It was the sound of water, of a steaming geyser, pushing its way from the bowels of the earth. He thought of his last experiment, the woman in the sensory deprivation laboratory. Something was doing to him what he had done to her. He was being deprived of his senses and even as he thought of this, he was aware of a dreadful smell, the stink of excrement. He held his breath to banish it, and another of his senses became redundant.

Half blind, deafened, choking on the smell, he was dragged slowly to the edge of the well, and now he became aware through his battered eardrums of a gurgling sound, water churning, the sound of waves crashing against rocks and the sucking noise of water gurgling back into itself. Gradually he was forced to his knees and he stared into the well, his eyes adjusting quickly to the blackness of the water which was curdling against the crumbling brickwork.

Beneath the surface he could make out a shape,

something human being swept up from the depths towards him. He could not move. He tried to turn away from the sight but he was no longer in control of his body. He tried to close his eyes but they remained stubbornly open.

The shape took on the form of a man, heavy and bloated, spiralling towards the surface.

No, please God, no. Just a hint of his voice, pleading, a small sound against the roar of the water, and then the thing had burst the surface of the water and grabbed him, the face inches from his, a gargoyle of a face, eyeless, just black empty sockets, and a leering toothless mouth, breath like cordite, the bloated skin breaking up and putrefying as he looked at it.

He screamed but the sound died instantly as he was dragged into the water, feeling himself being pulled into the depths and as he sank, his brain continued to torture him, continued to function after his eardrums had burst under the pressure. It was the face Melanie had described to him on the phone before she died, a very vision of hell, she had called it, but the knowledge gave him no comfort, even as his lungs filled with putrid water. And still his brain tortured him. Starved of oxygen, it produced a final note of irony. As he died, Elliot West was aware that for the first time in his life, in the last seconds of his existence, he had come to believe in Hell . . .

Baxter had lost all track of time. He had no idea how long it had taken him to make his way up the two flights of stairs, each step a colossal effort against the freezing gale. The whole house had frozen. He dared not touch the walls in case his hand stuck to them. Finally he reached the attic door and pushed it open with his shoulder. Something was obstructing it. He pushed harder and it moved a couple of inches. Wedging himself into the crack, he heaved again and stumbled inside.

The obstruction was Nancy, lying slumped against the door in the foetal position. Bending over her, he had a flash of memory, of Melanie in the same position on the day he had found her, trying to make herself as small as possible.

As he pulled her to her feet, he was aware of a crackling sound, like ice breaking, then he caught sight of her face and shuddered in horror. She was covered in an extra skin of frost. Frantically he began to scrape it from her face, tearing chunks of it from her arms, the ice sticking to his fingers then breaking off, taking a layer of skin with it.

He shook her and shouted her name. Her eyes were open but there was no spark in them. She gazed blankly over his shoulder; just as Susan had done.

Again he yelled her name, trying to rouse her, then he turned as the plaster behind him began to crack; a diagonal fissure from floor to ceiling. Floorboards creaked and two boards sprang free of the joists and snapped against the wall. Through the gap he could see his bedroom below and then plaster fell from the ceiling, a snowstorm of plaster, covering him in flakes. Timbers groaned and the masonry screamed, bricks grinding against one another. The house was tearing itself apart.

'Nancy!' He was yelling at her now, slapping her face and rubbing her hands. Her flesh was cold and damp, like putty. He pleaded with her in the name of God, then instinctively began to recite the twenty-third psalm.

'Yea, though I walk through the valley . . .' He could not remember the words. 'Thy rod and thy staff they comfort me . . .'

Her eyelids fluttered and he gave thanks to God, then turned as a second gap opened in the wall behind him. It was big enough to see through. He could look out into the night but there was nothing to be seen. Ocean Avenue was a black void, featureless and empty.

He hoisted her over his shoulder like a sack of coal, dragged her to the landing and down the first step, almost slithering on the ice. The staircase was a toboggan run of ice. He grabbed the banister and felt the ice burn his hand and, when he dragged it free, he left skin behind, a triangular flag of skin, fluttering in the gale.

Bleeding, tiptoeing like a ballet dancer, he made his way down. On the last step he fell against the wall, cushioned by Nancy's body. He heard her grunt in pain and he gave thanks, for it meant that she was still with him, still alive.

The ground floor was a disaster area. Turning his face to the wall to avoid looking at the bodies and to prevent the nausea rising in his gullet, he made his way down the second flight to the hall. He could no longer see the front door. It had vanished behind a wall of ice. Propping Nancy against the staircase, he ran towards the door. It had gone, torn from its hinges. Through the ice, he could see the shimmering forms of the survivors, a small group standing motionless, staring back at him. He turned and looked into the living room, searching for an exit. The shattered window had iced over and he could see the jagged outline of glass embedded in the ice. It was better to take a chance with the doorway.

Backing off a few feet, he ran at it, head and shoulders down. Moving like a running back, he smashed into it, felt it crack. He turned and snatched a glance at Nancy. Were it not for the ice forming on her face she could have been the picture of contentment, asleep on the stairs, her face girlish, composed.

For her sake, he said to himself. If not for me, then for Nancy. Again he hurled himself at the ice, both feet off the ground, head first into the ice. Concussed he burst through and fell on to the gravel. For a moment he lay stunned, then his eyes focused. The gap was icing up again. He scrambled to his feet, pushed his way back through and ran to Nancy. There was no time to try to wake her. He dragged her by the arms across the floor, hit the ice for the third time and they were through, spraying icicles before them, out into the sweet air and he was half lifting, half dragging her across the gravel to the trees where the others stood, ghostly in their white suits, some of them smeared with blood, each one wearing the blank, featureless expression of men and women in shock.

'Where's Elliot?' he yelled, looking from one face to the other, searching for him.

One of the young men shrugged and pointed to his left, muttered that he was trapped in the basement.

Baxter grunted an obscenity. He wanted to shake them out of their lethargy, slap them into action, but there was no time. Gently he lay Nancy on the ground and ran round the corner to the storm door. It was solid with ice, as solid as reinforced steel. He bent low and looked through the bars, whispering West's name. He could see no sign of life, just the open well. It was smoking, sending a cloud of black smoke to the ceiling.

'Elliot,' he roared, grabbing at the iron bars, his

hands sticking to them, glued to the ice. His voice was that of an animal, roaring, a mixture of pain and frustration, screaming his friend's name, the tears beginning to cloud his vision, then he was silent as the first flame burst out of the well.

He gaped at it, thinking that he could detect the contours of a face in the flickering flame, a ghastly face, grotesque. It reached out for him and he felt it singe his face. Yelping with pain he threw himself back, his hands tearing on the bars, then squatted like a dog on all fours, staring through the window. In a matter of seconds, the well had become a volcano, roaring and belching a column of flame up both staircases, towards the storm door and the living room.

He felt a tremor in his fingers and toes and began to crawl away from the window as the first explosion roared through the house.

The technicians shrank back from him as he pushed through them, a grotesque sight, face blackened, eyebrows burned off, his hair smoking, hands bleeding and raw.

Nancy had propped herself against a tree and looked up at him as he bent over her.

'She's gone,' she said softly. 'Susan's gone. She's not there anymore.'

He reached for her and she clung to him, returning the embrace. For a full minute they held on to one another, united in grief, until a communal gasp from the others made them turn. The house was a mass of flames now, reaching as far as the two half-moon windows. Briefly the window panes glinted down at them, blinking at them, then exploded simultaneously in a cascade of sparks, sending splinters of glass into the black night sky and showering the gravel with shrapnel. A young woman screamed as she was hit, and Baxter grunted with hatred, thinking that, even as it died, the house was still on the attack, still trying to maim and kill.

Now the flames split in two, running up both sides of the house to meet above it, flickering like the fingertips of lovers reaching out for each other, then meeting in an embrace as the roof collapsed, spewing smoke, the sparks spiralling towards them. Instinctively the crowd stepped back from the smouldering grass, all except Baxter and Nancy who stood together, defying the house to hurt them any more.

'It's almost over,' he whispered. 'Hell is reclaiming its own.'

They stood motionless, spectators at an exorcism by fire.

'Ashes to ashes,' said Nancy. Baxter muttered an amen and they turned away from the scene of destruction. Arm in arm, lost in one another, they did not notice the doll on the grass, a bald, scarred, one-eyed doll smiling up at them.

Baxter trod on it and it moaned, 'Mama, Mama . . .' but the tiny voice was lost in the roar of the flames and they heard nothing; nor did they see a large fly land on the doll's mouth.

Slowly the face began to frost over until the glass eye cracked. Only then did the fly move, its wings and body shimmering with frost, following them, a yard from Baxter's head.

And in the heat of the night, Baxter shivered.